CYNTHIA HICKEY

Deceptive Peace

Cynthia Hickey

To everyone who loves a good suspense with a hefty dose of romance. .

Chapter One

Her mother had once told her that Misty Hollow was the perfect place for someone to go who didn't want to be found. Sierra Wells wanted to disappear off the face of the earth.

When her mother had dropped the bombshell that the man Sierra almost got engaged to was actually her half-brother, a baby she'd given up for adoption, well...What a secret her mother had kept the eleventh hour. What if she'd died before letting Sierra know?

She pounded the steering wheel. Dear brother Dayton accepted the fact less graciously than Sierra had and said it made no difference to him. Sierra was his.

How dare he? She belonged to no one but herself. Only now, he'd grown violent, and she'd fled to the middle of absolutely nowhere, a town deep in the Ozark mountains. Talk about insane.

The car's headlights barely cut through the inky darkness. A mountain road that time of night might not have been a good idea, but Sierra hadn't wanted to stay another day where her brother could get her in his claws. No, Misty Hollow sounded perfect to her, and she'd found the cutest little house online. She even had a job waiting for her at the local coffee shop.

Heavy clouds overhead released their burden making visibility less. Sierra slowed her speed and leaned forward as if she could peer through the spaces in the raindrops. She glanced at her GPS. Nothing between her and her new home but dirt roads branching off the one she drove on. She had no choice but to keep driving.

Something slammed into her front bumper sending her car spinning. Sierra screamed and stomped on the brake as the car skidded into a ditch. Her head snapped forward, colliding with the steering wheel.

She sat there, fighting to catch her breath. What had she hit? Please, God, don't let it be a person. Don't be stupid. Why would a person be out on a night like this? She had to go check.

She shoved her car door open and stepped into the downpour. She sloshed her way out of the ditch, slipping several times in the process, until she once again stood on firm ground. A doe, its neck at an odd angle, lay on the embankment. Sierra turned and searched the trees behind her.

Her heart dropped as a spotted fawn stepped from the trees. "I'm so sorry, little one." Her words broke on a sob. "We're both in a pickle now."

There was no way she'd get her car out of the ditch short of a tow truck. She slid down the hill to the ditch and fished her cell phone out of her purse. No reception. Should she start walking or hope another vehicle would come by? Could she trust anyone that stopped? She'd seen too many times on the news how a woman out alone vanished without a trace. She sat in the driver's seat out of the rain and turned off both the lights and the engine. Her car would be the trace, should she disappear. Unless a serial killer tow-truck driver came around.

She glanced up and screamed. A man stood near the dead doe.

He laid his rifle on the ground and held up his hands. "Are you okay?" His words barely pierced the pouring rain.

"There's a fawn!" She pointed. She was definitely not okay. She put a hand to her head, bringing her fingers back sticky. When she looked up again, the hooded man stood next to the car.

"You're bleeding." His voice was softer than she'd thought.

"Thank you, Captain Obvious. I'm sorry. I'm a bit shook up. I don't mean to be rude."

"Apology accepted. Come with me."

"Uh, you're a stranger."

"If I was going to harm you, I'd have done so already. I'm not going to let the doe go to waste. You'll have to lure the fawn. I live a mile into the woods."

She grabbed her purse and the overnight bag she'd tossed in the backseat and returned to the rain filled nightmare of a night. "Come on, darling. Follow your mama."

The man hefted the doe onto his shoulders with a grunt. "Grab my gun."

Okay. Maybe he really did mean her no harm. She picked up his weapon and obediently followed. "Will my car be alright out here?"

"Who is going to steal a wrecked vehicle?"

Point taken. She couldn't get over how fast he

moved with a deer on his shoulders. She'd never manage to drag it more than a few feet.

How much farther? Her feet sank into puddles with every step. Her bag grew heavier as the clothes inside got wet.

Finally, she could make out a light through the rain and followed the stranger into a small clearing. He marched to a cement slab, cut holes in the doe's legs, and reeled her up on some contraption.

"Go on in, take a shower, make yourself comfortable. I'll be skinning the deer for about half an hour."

"What about the fawn?"

"I'll have to take care of her until she's big enough to fend for herself."

"What's your name? I'm Sierra Wells."

"Spencer Thorne."

Dismissed, she entered the cabin. Masculine with plaid throws on leather furniture, a crude wooden table that looked handmade, a small but functional kitchen. Two doors stood closed on the opposite wall. The first one led to a bedroom with a rugged four-poster bed. The second was the bathroom. The whole cabin was as big as her mother's living room.

Sierra dug in her overnight bag for the least wet of her things and turned on the shower. Before getting undressed, she turned the lock on the door, then leaned against it. What was she doing? She ran from one crazy man straight into the home of a stranger. What if this Spencer was as unhinged as Dayton?

~

While he had been out hunting, Spencer hated to see a fawn orphaned. It wasn't the woman's fault, but he still had to squelch his anger at the sight of the poor animal watching him with big eyes.

Now, the woman was in his house. He didn't like people. Avoided them as much as he could, but he couldn't leave her on the side of the road. Even Misty Hollow had its kooks.

Once he finished skinning and cutting up the deer, he tossed the parts he couldn't eat into a wheelbarrow and carted them to the edge of his property for the wild animals to enjoy. Then, he entered the house to the sound of the shower. Hopefully, she wouldn't use all the hot water. He got his electricity from solar panels, not wanting to be connected to the grid in any way. Except for his cell phone. His one luxury.

He grabbed a can of condensed milk from the cupboard. The fawn wasn't the first orphan he'd had to care for. He poured the milk into a bowl and set it on the corner of the porch. Hopefully, the little thing would eat.

Satisfied he'd done all he could at the moment, he went to his room and changed into a pair of flannel pants and a tee-shirt. His stomach rumbled, reminding him he hadn't eaten in a while. He frowned at the sound of the shower still running. Shaking his head, he grabbed eggs and bacon from the fridge.

When Sierra emerged from the bathroom, he said, "Solar panels provide my power. Long, hot showers are a luxury I don't have."

Her eyes widened. "I'm sorry. I didn't know. Can I trouble you for a ride home?"

"Sorry. Truck needs a new battery. I have the battery, but I've been out in the deluge long enough tonight. You're welcome to eggs, bacon, and the couch."

"Do you have a drier?" She clutched her wet bag.

He shook his head, cracking eggs into a bowl. "Line dry."

She sighed and set the bag next to the couch. "I've rented a place in Misty Hollow. Fully furnished, thank goodness." She sat in one of the kitchen chairs. "I start a job at Still Brewin' on Monday."

Spencer wasn't good at small talk. Instead, he preferred silence, which is why he lived alone except for Buster. "Can you let my dog in? He wandered off while I was hunting."

"Absolutely." She jumped up and opened the front door.

Buster, a large mixed breed dog, entered and shook, spraying Sierra.

The outrage on her face made Spencer smile. He ducked his head to hide his amusement. "He's harmless unless you try to hurt me."

"What if you try to harm me?" She returned to her seat.

"He'd help." He ducked his head to hide the twitching of his lips, then glanced up again.

Her face paled, and she stared at her hands folded on the table in front of her. After a few minutes, she wondered the cabin looking at and touching his things. Pretty woman. Hair the color of honey that fell past her shoulders. Hazel eyes that reflected her emotions by changing from green to blue and every shade in-between. Petite and slender, but curvy in all the right places. The men in town would be swarming like ants to a piece of white bread.

"Here." He set a plate of bacon and scrambled eggs

on the table, then fixed a plate for himself.

"Why don't you have any pictures?" She sat across from him.

"No need."

"You look military. Are you?"

"Was."

She sighed and started eating. He didn't like to be rude, but conversation seemed a waste of time when he doubted he'd see her again unless they passed on the street. No sense in exchanging information. He liked his peace and solitude and wanted nothing to change.

"I'm moving to Misty Hollow to make a fresh start. Are the people friendly? What about the local police? Are they capable?"

He jerked his gaze toward her. "That's an odd question to ask. Are you bringing trouble to our town?"

"No." She lied. He could tell by the look in her eyes. "But I am a woman living alone."

"The sheriff used to be FBI. He's quite capable." He narrowed his eyes. For the first time in a long time he wanted to know more about a person. What really brought this woman to Misty Hollow?

He tossed a piece of bacon to Buster. "We've had our share of trouble, but Misty Hollow is a nice place to live."

"I like how secluded it is." She forked eggs into her mouth.

Another strange statement. The woman seemed to be hiding. From what or from whom? Don't get involved, Spencer. Pretty women were always trouble. Keep your distance. Her problems were not yours.

When they'd finished eating, he gathered the plates and carried them to the sink. "You can use the blanket on the chair. Go ahead and get some sleep. I wake early." He washed the dishes and stared out the window.

The rain had lessened. Good. He should be able to replace the battery in his truck in the morning and get Sierra out of his house.

He stopped at the sofa and stared into her sleeping face, noting tear tracks on her face that had left the hair near her temple damp. His heart lurched. The woman was hurting, and he'd always had a soft spot for hurting creatures.

DECEPTIVE PEACE

Chapter Two

Sierra woke to the aroma of brewing coffee. No sunlight streamed through the window. Spencer hadn't lied about getting up early. She glanced at her watch. Six a.m.

"Coffee?" Spencer asked.

"Yes, please." She sat up, shoving her hair out of her face. The sooner she got up, the sooner she'd retrieve her car and get home.

Spencer handed her a thermos of coffee and a granola bar. "Might as well get going. I've already changed the battery in my truck."

She blinked the sleep from her eyes and nodded, mumbling, "Early bird."

He chuckled. "Guess you're not." He hefted her bag over his shoulder and headed for the door.

After slipping on her shoes, Sierra grabbed her purse and gave chase, thankful it wasn't raining. She climbed into the seat of an older model truck she couldn't believe still ran. While he drove, she took the opportunity to study her Good Samaritan.

Hair the color of oak wood cut in a military style. Camouflage pants and a tight-fitting olive green tee-shirt. Just a bit of scruff on his chin and cheeks. Very handsome. Too bad she'd sworn off men for a while.

His denim-colored eyes flicked her way. "What?"

"Nothing." She removed the lid from her thermos and took a small sip of Hades hot coffee.

"Careful. It's hot."

"That's an understatement." She turned her attention to the thick woods on each side of the road. "Taking the road is a lot longer than walking."

"No shortcuts this way."

"Thank you. I appreciate your help. I don't know what I would have done if you hadn't come by."

"Walk, I guess. You were only five miles from town."

Would have been a long, wet hike. A tow truck already had her car pulled from the ditch and ready to go.

"I need my suitcases from the trunk." Before Sierra could get out, Spencer held out his hand.

"Keys. I'll get your things."

She dropped the keys into his hand, more than happy to let him lug her overstuffed suitcases. Knowing she needed to make a fast getaway, she'd stuffed as many of her clothes and mementos into the two large cases as she could and cleared out her bank account. Every dollar she had was in her purse. While she waited, she pulled up the rental house on her GPS. A cute little white house with over a hundred acres of cattle pasture behind it. Not her land, but at least it afforded her a bit of privacy.

"You're carrying a lot in those bags." Spencer returned to the truck.

"Too heavy for a man who carried a deer?" She arched a brow and smiled. "Here's the directions to my house. Do I need to follow the tow truck or can I visit them tomorrow?"

"I'm sure tomorrow is fine." He pulled back onto the road and followed the tow truck into town. When they reached an intersection, the tow truck went right, he turned left. A couple of blocks later, he turned into her driveway. "Cute place." He glanced at the neighbors. "You going to feel safe all alone here?"

"Yes." She narrowed her eyes. "Why wouldn't I?"

He shrugged and pierced her with a sharp gaze. "Because I think you're running from something. Or someone. A bad breakup?"

"Something like that." He'd never believe her if she told him. Besides, it was none of his business why she came to his town. She shoved open her door and headed for a hanging plant where the landlord said the key would be waiting.

Stretching, she snatched the key and unlocked the windowed front door. She stepped aside so Spencer could carry her bags inside. "The master bedroom is down the hall, last door on the left."

He marched down the hall, a suitcase in each hand. "Do you need to buy groceries?"

"Yes, but the landlord said there is a bike in the shed out back. I can use that." She smiled up at him. "Thank you for everything. Maybe I'll see you around."

"Maybe." He jotted down a number on a pad of paper hanging on the side of the fridge. "My cell. Call me if you need anything."

She nodded, anxious for him to leave, and antsy that she would be truly alone when he did. Silly, girl. Dayton would never find her here. She was safe to start a new life in a sleepy little town nestled in the Ozark mountains. "Thanks again." She waited by the front door.

"Stay safe." With a lingering look, he nodded, then returned to his truck.

Her hand trembled as she closed the door and turned the lock. She unpacked the still damp things from her overnight bag and tossed them in the dryer. She placed a box of her mother's papers on the top shelf of the closet. She didn't have the heart to go through them yet. She'd unpack the rest of her things later. Right now, her next concern was food and a visit to the bank.

An old-fashioned, but fairly new bicycle leaned against the wall inside a small shed behind the house. She smiled and climbed on, hanging her purse around her neck.

She felt like a child again as she rode down the side of the street, wind blowing in her hair. Her nose and cheeks grew chilled, but didn't lessen her enjoyment. People waved as she passed, curiosity on their faces. In front of the bank, she locked the bike to a light post and entered the building, ready to get a check for several thousand dollars out of her purse and in a safe place.

She caught a glimpse of a man in a hoodie when she exited the bank. Her heart leaped into her throat at his stance, so close to how Dayton stood. Shaking her head, she climbed back on the bike. Don't be stupid. He didn't know where she was.

Still, as she rode toward the grocery store at the end of the street, the hair on the back of her neck stood at attention. It would take more than a few days for her to stop looking over her shoulder.

As she locked the bike up again, she glanced down the street. No sign of the man in the hoodie. Chuckling at herself for being afraid when she had no need to be, she entered the grocery store and grabbed a basket.

~

Driving away from Sierra had been the hardest thing he'd ever done. She could say a million times that she wasn't in trouble, but his gut told him otherwise, and his gut was rarely wrong.

He turned the truck around in time to see her ride the bike away from her house. He followed at a safe distance. If she spotted him, she'd be annoyed, or frightened, but he needed to know she was fine.

When she stepped out of the bank and froze, his gaze followed hers to a man standing on the sidewalk across the street. He didn't seem to be watching Sierra, but he also didn't look as if he belonged. Not in front of a women's hair salon.

Sierra rode to the grocery store, Spencer following. He could use a few food items. It had been a while since he'd shopped. Hunting and canning didn't give him everything he needed.

He roamed the store, putting items in his basket, and found Sierra in the produce section. Eyes wide, stance rigid, she stared toward the swinging doors the employees used. "Sierra?"

She gasped and whirled, her hand going to her throat. "You scared me."

"Something else frightened you first. What is it?"

"Just my imagination." She forced a laugh and put a few bananas in her basket. "I can only carry two bags on the bike so need to be careful what I buy."

"I can give you a ride home." He glanced at the

door. Eyes peered out, then ducked. "I'm not letting you go back alone. I'm taking you home, and you are going to tell me what you're running from." She'd look terrified when he'd approached.

Her brows lowered. "My life is not your concern."

"It is if you're in danger."

"If I'm in danger, I'll go to the police."

Aware they were starting to attract attention, he lowered his voice. "I really don't like getting involved in other people's lives, but that changed when you hit that deer and needed me."

"I no longer need you." She lifted her chin.

"Malarkey!" She had to be the most infuriating woman he'd ever met. "Either you tell me or I'll have the sheriff pay you a visit and you can tell him."

"You're a brute."

"What's your decision?"

"Fine. Take me home." She marched to the front of the store, exchanged her basket for a cart, and proceeded to fill it up.

He suspected she took her time just to irk him. Rather than complain, he followed her like an obedient puppy. Just before his patience ran out, she approached the register. While she paid, he searched the other customers. No one seemed overly interested in either of them. Maybe it had been her imagination that froze her in place in the produce section.

Thankfully, she didn't live far because the stony silence coming from the other side of the passenger seat could drive a man insane. "I'll help you with your groceries."

"Thank you." Back ramrod straight, she marched to the front door and unlocked it. "May I at least put the food away before you interrogate me?"

"It's not going to be like that." He set the bags on the table. Why was he so concerned about a woman who didn't want him to be? Because he had never walked away from someone needing him before and didn't plan to start now.

He sat at the table and drummed his fingers thinking of all the work waiting for him at home. The last of the garden to harvest, wood to be chopped for the coming winter, and here he sat. Idle.

"Would you like some coffee? A soda?"

"Water is fine." He folded his hands in front of him. He exhaled heavily, knowing she stalled for time.

She plopped a glass of ice water in front of him, then sat down. "Ask away."

"Who are you running from?"

"My half-brother."

"Why?" He watched her face over the rim of the glass.

Pain flickered in her eyes. "Seems my mother had a big secret. When I took Dayton to meet her and let her know we were getting married, she informed me—"

"Hold on. You were going to marry your brother?" He widened his eyes.

"I didn't know he was my brother." She clutched her water glass so tight her knuckles turned white. "Anyway, she told me who he really was. I broke off the engagement, of course. Was having second thoughts anyway. Dayton didn't take it as well. Said it didn't matter. That I was his, end of subject."

Spencer reached across the table and lay his hand over hers. "Did he hurt you?"

"Slapped me around a little. Tried to do more to

really make me his, his words, not mine, but I hit him over the head with a crystal vase and ran. He shouted after me that he would find me. My mother once said that Misty Hollow was the perfect place to disappear."

He felt as if he'd been punched in the gut. "How does your mother know about this town? If she mentioned it to you, she might have told your brother, too."

"I don't know how she knew. Research maybe." She paled. "Do you think he's here?"

"I don't know, but you need to think of every angle. I think we should pay a visit to the sheriff and see what he thinks. Where is your mother now?"

"She's dead. She lost control of her car. The police believe she was so upset over the news she gave me that she wasn't paying attention." She locked gazes with Spencer. "I think Dayton killed her."

"Do you have anything to back up that theory?"

"The look on his face when he heard the news. He was at my house, trying to convince me that my mother lied when the police arrived with the news." Her hands started to shake around her glass. "This was before he turned violent. He looked pleased, satisfied, when the officer told us."

"We're going to the local animal shelter and getting you a dog. You don't need to live alone."

Chapter Three

Spencer had Sierra in front of Sheriff Westbrook so fast her head spun. The speediness with which he acted and his palpable worry, had her hands shaking.

"Are you sure this Dayton Long is in Misty Hollow?" The sheriff's features grew grave.

"Not one hundred percent." Spencer reached over and placed a calming hand on Sierra's.

Warmth coursed through her, leveling out her breathing. "The hooded man stood the same."

The sheriff nodded. "I'll ask around town if there are any newcomers other than yourself and send a patrol car past your house a few times during the night. Until we know for sure that you're in danger, there isn't much else we can do. We're a small department of only a handful of officers."

"Thank you." Spencer stood, still holding her hand, and pulled her up beside him. "We're headed to the shelter to get her a dog."

"Good idea." The sheriff grinned. "I did the same thing for my wife once. No better warning system than a dog."

Sierra wanted to ask why his wife had needed a

dog, but Spencer was already leaving the room.

Outside, he opened the passenger side door. "Let me buy you lunch before we head to the shelter. We'll take a booth by the window and keep an eye out for this Dayton."

She didn't want lunch. She wanted peace and safety. Both of which she thought she'd find in Misty Hollow. But, she nodded, and got into his truck.

"You'll love Myrtle's. Most folks eat at least one meal a week there."

"Do you?"

He shook his head. "I try to stay to myself as much as possible."

"Getting involved with me has messed that up for you." She still didn't understand why he would go to so much trouble for a stranger, but his presence kept her from losing control and becoming a complete basket case. She clenched her hands together and stared out the window for a sight of the hooded man.

Myrtle's Diner sat on the corner of Main Street. Several cars were parked out front, causing Spencer to find a spot several doors down. "Saturdays are always busy." He cast her a worried look. "It will be okay."

"I don't know how he could have found me." She met his gaze. "Considering Mom never came straight with his identity until I told her we were getting married, I don't think they got along. I'd never seen him until I met him at a party. During that conversation…" the one that forever changed her life, "…Mom said she'd given him up for adoption."

"And that triggered this behavior." He held the door to the diner open for her.

"Yes." Then Mom had been killed before any kind

of reconciliation could occur.

"Somewhere in his crazed mind, Dayton has to know the two of you can't be together." Spencer motioned to a booth by the window.

The hostess nodded and grabbed two menus, following us to the booth. "Lucy will be your server." She placed the menus on the table and returned to her place by the door.

A knot formed in Sierra's stomach. The large window left her exposed to anyone watching, and she pressed against the back of the seat in an attempt to hide.

"Breathe, Sierra." Spencer locked gazes with her. "This is all precaution. He probably isn't here. You're right. Your mother wouldn't have spoken to him about this, not after mentioning it to you. She wouldn't have put you in danger that way."

True. Some of the tension melted from her shoulders. Mom must have seen Dayton's dark side and knew Sierra would have to flee. She opened her menu and scanned what she could order. A chef salad sounded good.

"That's it?" Spencer looked taken back. "You can get that anywhere."

"I can get a burger anywhere, too."

"Not like Myrtle's."

She tilted her head, a smile teasing at her lips. "I thought you didn't eat here often."

"I don't, but when I do I get the chicken fried steak with potatoes and gravy or a half-pound burger with mushrooms and cheddar."

What a difference a day made. Last night, Spencer had boarded on surly, today he acted as if the two of them were old friends. This charming Spencer could be far more dangerous than the one who'd treated her as an imposition just hours ago. She didn't want to get involved with a man anytime soon. Her heart still ached from what she'd thought to be love, only to find out she'd been delusional. What she'd thought she had wouldn't be easy to get over.

She'd fled home feeling very much in control of her life. Thinking Dayton might have followed her turned all that upside down. She much preferred the confident Sierra over the frightened one and would fight to get her confidence back.

"What's going through your head?" Spencer pulled her from her thoughts.

"What can I get you?" Lucy smiled down at them.

"A salad and a diet soda for me, extra dressing, please." Sierra handed her the menu.

"Chicken fried steak." Spencer tossed Sierra a wink.

Lucy promised to return with their drinks shortly.

"Your head?" Spencer arched a brow.

"It's nothing really. I'd left home with a goal in mind, plans to start a new life away from everything I'd ever known, and now that might be in danger of being the same thing I was running from." She shredded a napkin. "It's a little disturbing."

"We'll keep a watch out." He glanced out the window. "In small towns, if someone new shows up, everyone knows. If he's here, someone will tell us. No sense in worrying unless we know something."

~

Relieved to see some of the fear leave Sierra's face, Spencer straightened in his seat as the waitress brought their lunches. "Have you had a dog before?"

"No. With it being just me and mom, we didn't have money for a pet." She dumped a liberal amount of ranch dressing on her salad. "My friends had dogs." Her gaze flicked to the window again.

So, not completely worry free. Who knew an ordinary hunting trip would result in him getting involved with a complete stranger and trying to keep her safe? This wasn't him. He liked his solitude, his life with his dog. He cut into his meal. Spencer usually kept his head down. Sure, if he knew someone needed him, he'd help, but he sure didn't go looking for someone. This woman had dropped into his lap. So much for his peaceful life.

"What?" Sierra stared at him, the hand holding her fork halted halfway to her mouth.

"Just thinking."

"Care to share?" She moved the food to her mouth.

"Just dwelling on how things can change in the blink of an eye."

"Things being me."

He sat back and crossed his arms. "Well, yes."

"You don't have to help me, Spencer. I'm capable of taking care of myself."

"Do you have a gun?"

Her brow lowered. "No."

"Do you know how to shoot?"

"Yes." She huffed. "I do not want to own a gun."

"I think you should. We'll get you one before going to the shelter, which means we need to hurry before the shelter closes. I don't want you sleeping alone without a warning system."

"While I appreciate your help, you're getting

bossy. That is not okay. We just met, and I have one heavy-handed man in my life already." She slammed her fork on the table.

At first, he simply stared at her with wide eyes, then burst into laughter. "You've got spunk." He returned his attention to his meal. She'd need that stubbornness if her brother really had come to town.

When they finished eating, he paid the bill and drove Sierra to a local gun store and pawn shop. "I'm thinking a nine-millimeter Ruger. You should be able to handle a gun that size, and it'll fit in your purse."

"Whatever you say." High spots of color appeared on her cheeks.

"Are you still mad?"

She whirled to face him. "I never said I was mad."

"Then why the chilly tone in your voice?" He pulled the truck into an empty parking spot and cut the engine.

"I'm not happy with this chain of events. Get a dog, get a gun, you can't be alone, blah, blah, blah." She shoved her door open.

He got out on his side and caught up with her as she marched to the store door. "Am I wrong?"

"No, but I don't have to like it."

He reached around her to open the door, his arm brushing her shoulder. A spark shot up his arm. *Slow your roll, dude. No entanglements, remember? Help keep her safe and that's all. You've already been burned once. No need to go there again.*

Sierra marched to the counter and told the man what she wanted. "You might as well add that pink Taser and the pink military-style knife."

Spencer grinned. *Now, she was talking.* He

watched while she wrapped her fingers around the butt of the gun and aimed it at the wall. She knew what she was doing. Good. He'd sleep better knowing she took every precaution she could.

"That took a big chunk of my cash," Sierra said, purchases in her purse, as they returned to the truck. "Please stop spending my money. Today is turning out to be quite expensive."

He laughed, realizing that despite the gravity of the situation, he hadn't laughed this much in a very long time. "I promise."

The shelter echoed with barking dogs. He led her to the wing which housed the large ones.

Sierra strolled ahead of him, peering in cages and speaking softly to several of the animals until stopping in front of one and bending over to bring herself in eye level with a two-year-old German Shepherd/Lab mix. "Hello," she glanced at the card attached to the cage, "Annie."

The dog's tail thumped the concrete floor.

"Want to come home with me?" Sierra stretched out her hand for the dog to sniff. "I want this girl."

"I'll fetch the one in charge." He marched away, leaving her to get acquainted with the dog. He returned a few minutes later with the employee and a leash.

"So glad she found a home," the worker said. "The large dogs are harder to place."

"She's exactly what I need." Sierra took the leash and clipped it to Annie's collar.

"Next stop, pet store." Spencer led the way back to the truck, where Annie quickly jumped in and sat in the middle. Good thing his old truck had a bench seat.

"Thank you for suggesting a dog. My house won't

feel quite as lonely with this girl around."

"No, it won't. Dogs have a tendency to go everywhere you go. Even the bathroom. You'll have very little privacy." He grinned.

They made a quick stop at the pet store for food, dog dishes, a couple of toys, and a dog bed, before he drove her home. "Mind if I take a quick look around?"

"Go ahead." She unlocked the front door. "From now on, Annie will let me know if anything is amiss."

It didn't take long to check out the 1,000-square-foot house. He stepped out the kitchen door and surveyed the trees bordering her property. A person could easily sneak up without being seen. He'd come back tomorrow and install some motion lights. It might upset Sierra with him being "heavy-handed", but a woman a lone couldn't be too careful.

She opened the door and let Annie out. "Why so grave?"

He turned and told her about the lights. "That okay?"

She nodded. "I can see the sense in that."

His cell phone rang. "It's the garage." He pressed the speaker button. "Hello, Bob."

"Hey, Spence. You know that woman's car I towed in? You won't believe it, but I found a tracking device on the undercarriage."

Chapter Four

Sierra's knees sagged, and she put a hand against the wall to steady herself. Dayton was in Misty Hollow. He knew where she lived, what she drove.

"Come on." Spencer put an arm around her and led her to the sofa. "You're alright. You have Annie, and a gun. He can't take you by surprise. I'll go retrieve the tracking device and take it to the sheriff."

She nodded. "You're right. I'll keep the house locked. I've got Annie. I'll be fine." Would she, though? She knew in her heart he'd killed their mother. The obsession he had with Sierra wouldn't go away. He'd stalk her until somebody stopped him or he had her. She covered her face with her hands. "My mother was wrong. This isn't the place for a person to disappear."

Spenser knelt in front of her and pulled her hands away. "If not for the tracker…"

"Right. But, he did track me." She wanted to ask him to stay, but she refused to put anyone else in danger. There would come a day when she faced her brother again, and one of them wouldn't walk away. "I'll be fine. You checked the house. Go on home and thank you." She got to her feet and headed for the door.

He hesitated, then nodded. "I've got to care for Buster and the fawn. Call me if you need me. I'm only five miles away."

"I will." She forced a smile and held the door open. When he stepped out, she closed it and turned the deadbolt. "Well, girl. It's you and me now. Hungry?"

Annie thumped her tail.

Sierra forced her feelings of foreboding aside and took care of her new family member. "Hey, you're my only family member." She refused to consider her psycho half-brother as any relation. The knowledge brought burning tears to her eyes.

After the dog ate, Sierra poured herself a glass of wine and sat on the back patio while Annie explored the fenced yard. Dayton wouldn't take a sniper shot at her. He wanted her alive, so as long as Annie didn't give the alarm, Sierra would enjoy the hours before bedtime. Soon, the weather would be too cold to enjoy a drink on the patio.

Her gaze studied the tree line over the rim of her glass. Not real thick, but there were a few ancient trees with trunks large enough for someone to hide behind. They couldn't approach the house without being seen though.

Tomorrow, she'd buy some cameras that would send an alert to her phone if someone passed by them. Pleased with being proactive instead of a trembling mess, she relaxed. She was no longer stunned by her mother's news. Now, she'd fight to have the life she wanted. One of independence, peace, and someday a husband and family. She would not let Dayton ruin that for her.

When she finished her glass, she carried it in the

house and called for Annie to follow. "Time for bed, girl." She locked the back door, checked the front door and windows, then headed for bed.

Despite her dog bed on the floor, Annie hogged most of Sierra's bed during the night. "Naughty dog." Sierra smiled. It had been nice not to sleep alone.

After a shower and quick breakfast, Sierra took Annie for a walk. It being a Sunday, the stores weren't open that early. She'd have to wait another hour before getting her cameras.

"Welcome to town." An elderly woman with a floppy hat on her head, leaned on a shovel. "I'm Maggie."

"Sierra, and this is Annie. Nice to meet you."

"You'll like it here. We've a nice town with little crime. Mostly teenagers causing mischief. You alone?"

"Yes. I'll be working at Still Brewin' Coffee Shop starting tomorrow."

"Oh, then, you'll meet most of the town. Well, the younger crowd. Us older people, except a group of old men who like to chat while they drink their coffee, like Myrtle's."

Sierra glanced up and down the street. "Is there anyone else new to town?"

The woman scrunched her face. "Not that I know of, and I know a lot of what goes on around here. But, if they rented a cabin on the mountain, I might not know. The realty company would."

Sierra would check with them on her lunch break tomorrow. "I'll let you get back to your flowers."

She strolled to the edge of Main Street, not wanting to leave her residential neighborhood just yet, then turned around and took Annie home. "I'll be back soon."

She retrieved her bike from the shed and cruised to the general store which promised to carry everything you couldn't buy at the grocery store. She hoped their claim was right.

After locking the bike to a lamppost, she entered the store. A bell jingled over her head, bringing a middle-aged man with a bald head and round face to the counter. "How may I help you?"

"I'm looking for indoor/outdoor cameras that run off Wi-Fi and connect to my phone. Would you have any? I'd like four." Two for inside, and two for outside.

"You betcha. They're real popular and not any bigger than a six-ounce steak. Be right back." He returned with four boxes and set them on the counter. "Two-hundred-dollars."

Sierra winced, but handed the man her credit card. Since she needed them, she'd have to pay whatever they cost.

She left the store, hung the bag on her handlebars, and rode past the garage. Seeing the mechanic, she stopped. "Any idea when my car will be finished?"

"It's drivable right now, but that new bumper won't be in for at least a week."

"Okay. I can get everywhere I need on the bike. Thanks. Oh, and call me when it's finished, not Spencer. Okay?" She smiled and continued on her way.

Luckily, the backyard shed contained a ladder and the instructions to the cameras were easy to follow. See? She was perfectly capable of looking out for herself. An hour later, she had the cameras installed and settled down to watch a romantic comedy on television.

~

Dayton paced the hunter's cabin he'd chosen to live in until someone threw him out. How could Sierra sit there, sipping wine last night, as if she didn't have a care in the world? She belonged to him. Didn't she realize that? Her mother had lied about them being brother and sister. He'd feel it in his heart if they were. Why had the old witch lied like that?

And who was the hick driving her around? She couldn't possibly have replaced Dayton that quickly. He punched the log wall. Pain radiated through his knuckles. If she had, they'd both pay. Either she belonged to Dayton or no one.

He pressed his hands around his head and squeezed. Why had that woman ruined his life? His mother? Hah. No real mother, no good mother, gave up their first-born son. Blood related to Sierra? He didn't care. He didn't want kids anyway.

His head ached with a vengeance, sharp shards of glass piercing his brain. The doctor said he only had a few months. He intended on spending those months with Sierra.

~

After a restless night, Spencer had to force himself not to call and check up on Sierra. The day before, she seemed to want to manage things on her own. He would respect her wishes, no matter how hard it was. To take his mind off her, he grabbed his gun, called to Buster, and set out to go hunting.

A nip in the air signaled the arrival of fall. His favorite season because of hunting. The deer were getting over-populated on the mountain, and he knew several elderly people on a fixed income that could use the meat.

He'd stop occasionally and wait to see if a deer crossed his path. Usually, he went hunting a lot earlier in the day. But, he'd overslept, something he rarely did. Another thing that had changed with Sierra's arrival.

A cabin appeared through a break in the trees. "Hello, the cabin!" Not wanting to get shot, he shouted a warning. When he didn't receive a response, he approached the porch.

He motioned for Buster to go first. The dog bounded up the steps and nudged the door open. Spencer glanced at the broken handle on his way in.

A sleeping bag lay in the corner by a woodburning stove. A couple of bags of prepared food sat near a case of bottled water. The cabin had existed on the mountain for as long as Spencer could remember and provided shelter for many hunters each year.

"Come on, boy. Let's not bother anything. Whoever is staying here will be back." Spencer didn't want a bullet in his back or Buster's from a trigger-happy hunter.

He returned to his own cabin, still restless. "This is ridiculous." He shed his orange vest and grabbed his truck keys. "I'm heading into town to get a burger from Myrtle's. Hold down the fort." He patted his dog's head. He needed to drive by Sierra's place to make sure she was okay, even if he didn't stop. On the drive, he put his phone on speaker and called the sheriff.

"This is Spencer Thorne. The mechanic working on Miss Wells's car found a tracking device. I think it's safe to say her stalker is in town."

Sheriff Westbrook sighed. "I'll increase drive-bys at her house as often as I can spare an officer. We're a small force here. You know that."

"I appreciate it. Thanks. I'll bring the tracker by the station tomorrow." He hung up and drummed his fingers on the steering wheel. Would Sierra move to his cabin for her safety? He wanted to ask, but knew she'd decline.

He slowed, spotting Sierra on her front porch. She caught him cruising by, put her hands on her hips, and tilted her head. Busted. He stopped and rolled down the window. "I'm headed to Myrtle's, want to come?"

"What happened to rarely coming to town?"

"I didn't feel like cooking."

"Come on in. I've started supper and there's plenty." She entered the house without waiting for his reply, as if knowing he'd stay for supper.

He pulled into the driveway and cut the engine. After a quick glance around the yard, noting the outdoor cameras, he entered the house. "The cameras are a nice addition."

"Proactive." She grinned. "How does lasagna sound?"

"Perfect." Already, the kitchen smelled of cheese and marinara sauce. His stomach grumbled. "Any action on the cameras?"

"I installed them this afternoon. Other than a wasp, no. If I see anything of the two-legged variety tonight, I'll call the police." She tore lettuce into a bowl.

"Why are you making so much for supper?"

"I usually freeze half for nights I need something quick. Sometimes, I spend my Sundays cooking and freezing for the whole week. I hope to start doing that again next weekend."

"You're a lot calmer today." He pulled the cutting board with a tomato on it and started cutting.

"There's nothing more I can do, so why worry? I'll have plenty of warning if Dayton shows up. I'll always have my purse with me when I leave the house." She shrugged. "I'm not going to live my life in fear. I've done that long enough."

"How long?"

"Three weeks." She exhaled heavily. "Took me that long to get things squared away so I could leave. A lot of good that did, and I still left in a hurry."

She seemed so different from the woman of yesterday. This one was ready to face the danger head on when it came. Respect rose in Spencer, and a sense of pride came over him. He liked to think that his urging her to get a dog and a gun had spurred her to regain her confidence.

"Foods ready." She pulled the lasagna from the oven.

"Hmmm." The topping bubbled and the cheese had turned the most beautiful golden brown. "I haven't had a meal like this since I left home at the age of eighteen."

"I hope you enjoy it." She set the pan on potholders in the center of the table, then retrieved plates and silverware while he set the salad on the table.

Spencer reached for the spatula to cut into the lasagna when Sierra's phone dinged.

"That's the backyard camera."

Chapter Five

After discovering the camera the night before had been triggered by a raccoon, Sierra jerked awake at every little sound. Now, at far too early of an hour, she lay on her back and stared at the rotating ceiling fan. Her right hand absently petted Annie.

There'd been no reason to not sleep well. A lovely dinner with Spencer, then some time spent reading. Annie hadn't acted as if there was anything to worry about. Wasn't that why Sierra had a dog?

She groaned and tossed aside the blankets. Might as well start her day. She had two hours until she started her new job.

After a long, hot shower, she poured herself a cup of coffee and stepped on the back porch while Annie nosed around the yard. Maybe she could angle the camera to pick up creatures taller than a raccoon.

A glance at her watch alerted her she needed to be on her bike and headed to Still Brewin'. She promised Annie she'd be back later, locked up the house, and then headed to work. Maybe she did need her car. The autumn nip in the air froze her cheeks.

As she rode, she glanced around her constantly for sight of Dayton. What would she do if she saw him? Be late her first day at work so she could confront him? She shook her head in an attempt to get her mind where it needed to be. If all he did was watch her, she'd continue as if his presence didn't bother her. But, she would definitely acknowledge that he was there.

She locked up her bike and opened the door to Still Brewin'.

"You must be Sierra." The barista said. "I'm Sue Ellen. Nice to meet you." The softly plump blond smiled across the coffee shop. "Ready to get started?"

"Very much." As the day progressed, Sierra realized how nice the people of Misty Hollow were. Somehow, many of them had found out a new girl would start that day and flocked to the coffee shop to say howdy.

"About time we got a new pretty face around here," one man who looked to be over eighty said.

"That's sweet." Sierra poured him a small black coffee.

"You here permanently?"

"Yes, sir, I'd like to think so."

"Good." He flashed a grin that missed several teeth, then sat at a table where other elderly men in overalls sat.

Sierra glanced several times at the door, hoping to see Spencer enter. How silly. The man had a life of his own. He'd helped her all he needed to. She shouldn't expect to see him every day. But, since he'd mentioned taking the tracking device to the sheriff, she'd expected him to at least stop in to say hello.

During her lunch break, she strolled around the block to the realtor's office. A well-dressed woman sat behind a desk and glanced up with a smile when Sierra entered. "Welcome to Misty Hollow Realty and Rental Management. May I help you?"

"You already have. I'm Sierra Wells. I rent a house on Elm Street."

"Oh, yes. How are you settling in?"

"Just fine. I love the house. I'm wondering if you can tell me whether there are any other newcomers to town?"

"Looking to meet like-minded people?" She tilted her head.

"Something like that."

"Unfortunately, you're the only recent newcomer that I know of."

So much for that idea. "Thank you." She stepped back outside and scanned the street. Where are you, Dayton?

She narrowed her eyes at a man marching in the opposite direction. His build and the way he walked looked like Dayton.

"Hey."

She jerked, startled. "Hey, yourself." She smiled up at Spencer. "Get the tracking device turned in?"

"Yep. Went by the coffeeshop but they said you were on your lunch break."

She nodded, way too pleased that he'd looked her up. "I asked at the realtor's office whether any newcomers had come to town. No one but me."

"You seemed miles away when I approached you."

"I thought I might have seen Dayton."

"Following you?"

"No, walking away. I've got to get back to work."

"I'll go with you." He glanced to where she'd been staring. "I hope you didn't have any notions of confronting him."

She laughed. "I did for a second, but realized how stupid that would be."

"Good." He placed his hand on the small of her back. "Because stupid doesn't fit you."

Tingles shot up her spine. Yes, she enjoyed his company way more than she should, especially since her broken engagement had occurred only a month ago, and she'd just met Spencer. But had she really loved Dayton or been in love with the idea of marriage? He'd always been a little…bossy.

She glanced up at Spencer. Also bossy, but in a different way. A way she couldn't explain and while annoying at times, didn't cause anxiety. How could she not have seen the evil in Dayton?

When they arrived back at the coffee shop, she wanted to ask Spencer what he was going to do for the rest of the day. Wanted to invite him for supper again. Instead, she told him to have a good day and went back to work.

~

Dayton had hoped Sierra would follow him. He'd felt her eyes on his back. Then, when he turned the corner, the stupid hick had been with her. He'd spent time at her house the evening before. How quickly she'd gone from him to another.

He'd make her pay for leaving him. Anger quickened his steps. He'd parked his car a couple of streets over, near a cornfield, so he wouldn't attract a lot of attention. People in small towns were too nosy for their own good.

Dust rose above the field freezing him in place. Seconds later, a tractor emerged from around the field.

Spotting Dayton, the heavy-set man turned off the engine.

"You lost, mister? That your vehicle?"

Dayton reached for the gun in his waistband. "No, sir. My apologies."

"For what?"

"This." Dayton put a bullet between the man's eyes. "No witnesses." He climbed into his car and set the gun on the passenger seat before speeding away from the town. Someone would have heard the gunshot.

~

Spencer whirled at the sound of a gunshot, his hand suspended mid-air as he'd reached for his truck's door handle.

"That sounded like it came from Hank's cornfield," someone said. "You can't shoot that close to city limits."

Spencer hadn't lived to the age of thirty without trusting his gut. Instinct told him something foul had happened. "Get the sheriff. I'll head over that way."

The man nodded and lumbered toward the sheriff's office.

Spencer raced for the cornfield, skidding to a stop in the dirt on the side of the road, far enough away from the scene so he wouldn't contaminate anything. Hank lay slumped over the steering wheel of his tractor, the back of his head gone. Spencer tensed, studying the area.

There. A car had sped away. He studied the tire tread. Looked standard to him, but he was no crime scene tech. He glanced up as the sheriff's car pulled behind his.

"Poor Hank." Sheriff Westbrook shook his head.

"Why would someone shoot him? Everyone loved the man. You see anything, Spence?"

"No. The shooter was gone when I arrived."

The sheriff's face darkened. "Could be the guy following Miss Wells. He could've been here, Hank saw him, and...well, he knew word would spread about a new face in town. It's only a theory at this point."

"Sierra did think she saw him this afternoon. Not positive, though." His hands curled into fists. "I'd rather she not know we suspect Dayton Long to have killed."

"I understand. Why worry her without further proof." He stared down the road. "I don't like thinking this man is killing off my town's people. I'd rather it be someone passing through. If it is Long, others will die because of his obsession with Miss Wells."

Spencer nodded. The idea didn't sit well with him either. Someone passing through wouldn't leave a trail of death. Long might.

"I hate to have to tell his wife." He turned as a van pulled up. "Crime scene techs. You're free to go, Spence, since you didn't see anything. Keep a close watch on Miss Wells."

"I will." He trudged back to his truck and got in. How could he watch Sierra without her feeling stifled? He didn't even know what time she got off work. Drumming his fingers on the steering wheel, he contemplated his next move.

With a sigh, he turned the truck toward the coffee shop and parked in front of the drugstore. He had a clear view of the front door Sierra would exit, but doubted she'd notice him. Hopefully, she got off soon.

While he waited, he studied every man that moved

down the street. If anyone acted the least bit suspicious, he'd snap a photo of them with his phone and send it to the sheriff. His stomach rumbled, reminding him he hadn't had lunch.

He called the local pizza parlor. "I'd like a mega meat pizza delivered to the blue truck in front of the drugstore on Main Street. Oh, and a large soda."

"You want it delivered to a truck?"

"Yep." He grinned, pretty sure this type of delivery would be the driver's first.

"Okay. It'll be there in less than thirty minutes."

The pizza arrived in twenty-five minutes. Spencer gave a large tip and settled back to enjoy his meal while watching the coffee shop.

Several folks passing by would send him curious glances. A few who knew him asked why he was eating in his truck on Main Street. He said he was taking a break from running errands which seemed to satisfy them.

When he'd finished the pizza, he got out of his vehicle and threw it in the nearest trashcan. A black sedan drove down the street, slowing as it got close to Spencer.

The man inside raised a gun.

Spencer dove to the ground as a shot rang out.

The car continued past.

Spencer jumped up and rushed to the driver's seat, ignoring all the curious looks cast his way and shouts of, "Are you okay?" No way was this guy getting away from him. He turned the key in the ignition and roared from his parking spot, narrowly hitting another vehicle.

The car honked, flipped him the middle finger, and slammed on its brakes. Spencer waved a hand in apology and increased his speed. With one hand, he called the sheriff, putting him on speaker.

"This is Spencer. A man in a black Corolla shot at me in front of the drugstore. I'm now in pursuit heading out of town and nearing the Interstate."

"Keep me updated, but do not engage. I'm sending patrol cars your way."

Spencer clicked off his phone and put both hands on the wheel. His truck might be old and rusty, but it had a good engine. Keeping up with the Corolla shouldn't be any trouble.

It turned out to be harder than he'd thought. Long had no qualms about whipping in and out of vehicles on the Interstate. Spencer drove more carefully, not relishing getting into an accident and hurting an innocent driver.

Long had escalated quickly, killing the farmer, then shooting at Spencer. Why target Spencer? Did he know about his helping Sierra? He must've seen them together in town.

He slapped the steering wheel. This insane fool wouldn't stop until he had her. Spencer would not let that happen.

Long took an exit ramp, then turned left.

Spencer followed and…lost him. Sirens wailed behind him as two squad cars, lights flashing, pulled alongside him. He shrugged and pointed left. As the police cars went in search of Long, Spencer drove to the access ramp and back toward Misty Hollow.

There'd be no keeping the secret of Long's violence from Sierra now.

Chapter Six

"Did you hear about Hank? He's dead. Shot between the eyes." A middle-aged man darted into the coffee shop, then right back out like Paul Revere warning about the English coming.

Sue Ellen gasped. "Who would want to shoot Hank? What a tragedy."

"Was it that loud pop we heard?" Sierra moved to the window.

"I don't know." Sue Ellen grabbed her purse. "We'll know more outside. It's time to lock up anyway."

Sierra followed the other woman outside where a large crowd gathered. They all seemed interested in the drugstore across the street. "Is that where Hank was killed?"

A man standing nearby answered. "No. He was out by his cornfield. This is where someone took a shot at Spencer Thorne."

Spencer? She glanced around, standing on tip-toe in hopes of spotting him. "Was he hit?"

"Nope, but he looked mad as a rabid badger as he took off after the shooter. I almost feel sorry for the other guy if Spencer catches him."

She didn't. She hoped Spencer did catch whoever it was. Although, she had a strong feeling about who was behind the shootings. Hopefully, Spencer would wring his neck!

Spotting Spencer's truck coming down the street, she stepped away from the crowd and headed his way. He parked next to the curb and got out. As he approached her, his gaze locked on hers with an intensity that caused her heart to skip a beat.

"Are you okay?" She stared into worried eyes.

He put his hands on her shoulders. "I'm fine."

"Was it Dayton?"

"Pretty sure it was. I lost him, though. The police are searching for him. I think you need to come to the cabin with me."

"I'm not leaving my home. I'm safe there. I've got Annie and the cameras." But not him. She didn't have Spencer. "He shot at you, not me."

By now, the crowd surrounded them. Questions rang out.

Spencer took Sierra by the arm. "I don't know anything, folks. The guy got away." He led her to her bike. "I'm going to at least take you home."

Knowing arguing would do no good, she simply nodded and followed him to his truck. He stashed the bike in the back while she climbed in the passenger seat. "Are you hungry?" She cut him a glance.

"I ate a whole pizza in my truck." The corner of his mouth twitched.

"Recently?" She tilted her head. "Why would you eat it in your truck?"

"Uh…" He looked sheepish.

"Were you in the drugstore parking lot so you

could watch the coffee shop?" Her voice rose. "That's considered stalking, Spencer." She crossed her arms and glared out the window.

He might not have attacked her like Dayton had, but watching her every move bordered on suffocating. Because of his actions, he'd almost gotten himself killed. Her insane half-brother must think her and Spencer a couple and wants to eliminate the competition. Danger toward Spencer had risen to new heights. Danger or not, he still intended to keep Sierra safe.

"I'm sorry," Spencer said softly. "After you saw Dayton on the sidewalk, then the farmer being killed, I got worried. I wouldn't put it past Dayton to storm into the coffee shop and hold the customers hostage until you agreed to go with him."

She whipped around to face him. "You think he would actually do that?"

He shrugged. "You know him better than I do, but it's possible, isn't it?"

"Maybe. He isn't the Dayton he was when we started dating. He started changing about a year ago and went completely nuts when my mother revealed her secret. I thought it was stress over his job."

"What kind of job?"

"He's a psychiatrist."

"Wow. Didn't expect that." He pulled into her drive. "Do you want me to leave?"

"No." She shoved open her door and headed for the house, confident everything would be fine. Her phone hadn't signaled anyone on the property other than Annie roaming thru the house. She unlocked the door to be greeted by her dog who wagged her tail so

hard she almost folded in half. Laughing, Sierra gave
her a hug, then opened the kitchen back door so the dog
could go out.

Spencer checked every room in the house before
taking a seat at the table. "Everything looks good."

"The cameras showed nothing. Coffee?"

"Sure, and you can't be too careful, Sierra. Dayton
has shown he'll kill to get what he wants."

A chill trickled down her spine as she measured
the coffee grinds. "I think I'm safer in this house than
you are in yours."

He laughed. "You might be right. Maybe I should
move in here."

She froze, then relaxed as she realized he was only
teasing. "And live on the grid? In town? You'd be
miserable. I'm surprised you have a cell phone."

"It's the one thing I allow myself."

"Why did you decide to live that way?"

"When I got back from Afghanistan the last time
and reenlistment came up, I decided I was tired of
fighting. So, I found a small mountain town and bought
a cabin and land. I've been here five years."

She poured him a cup of coffee grabbed a diet soda
from the fridge for herself. She set the coffee cup in
front of him and sat across the table. "I can understand
that."

"What did you do before coming here?"

"Same thing I'm doing now. That's actually how I
met Dayton. He came into the shop one day, bought a
drink, and came back every day until I agreed to go out
with him." She wrapped her hands around the soda can.
"He'd been very sweet once upon a time."

"You couldn't have married him. Not with him

being who he is."

"Oh, I know. I was falling out of love with him months ago. Mom's news was a shock, but gave me an easy way out. I thought." She wanted to ask him if he'd ever been married or gotten close, but bit her tongue. He was too quickly becoming someone important to her. Now was not the time to get her heart involved with anyone. Best not to know too much about him.

~

Had the hick really thought he could catch me? Dayton snarled. He'd left both him and the cops in his dust.

He tapped his temple. "I'm way too smart. These people have seen nothing like me." He might have a monster growing in his skull, one that would eventually win the battle, but Dayton still had his smarts. Too intelligent for anyone from this mountain town.

Raising binoculars to his eyes, he tried maneuvering the sight through trees so he could get a look inside Sierra's house. There. He zoomed in and cursed, catching a look of her and the man chatting and drinking coffee in her kitchen.

As familiar as she seemed to be with him, she had to have known him when she ran from Dayton. "Well, I might've missed you this time, buddy, but next time you won't be as lucky." Still, Dayton wasn't a very good shot. He'd been the lucky one with the farmer, standing close enough he couldn't miss. He'd have to find another way to get rid of the hick.

He raised the binoculars again as the two he watched, plus a big dog, stepped onto the back deck. When Dayton got tired of watching the man with the woman who belonged to him, he'd go in search of the hick's cabin. He had a fairly good idea where he lived, having run across a dirt road in good shape in his own search for a place to shelter.

~

Spencer followed Sierra to the back deck. The hair on the back of his neck stood at attention. Someone watched them from the safety of the trees. Too far away for Spencer to see, but he knew Dayton was there.

"What is it?" Sierra glanced in the direction he was looking.

"I feel as if someone is watching us." The hair on the back of Spencer's neck stood at attention. His stomach fluttered.

"Annie doesn't seem concerned."

"She hasn't seemed concerned since you got her." He leaned on the railing, keeping his eyes peeled for anything that moved.

"Don't you think we need a plan? We can't just wait for him to come for one of us. We should set a trap."

He narrowed his eyes and shook his head. "That's not a good idea. If we set a trap and it goes wrong, he's got you."

"So, sit and wait." She crossed her arms. "That doesn't sound any better. I want to live my life, Spencer, and not in fear. I could really grow to like this town."

"Let's give the sheriff a few days before deciding anything. They might find him." He started to reach for her hand and stopped.

Annie stood at attention, her hackles raised, and stared into the trees. He'd been right. Someone was definitely out there.

"Get inside, Sierra."

Her eyes widened. "Come, Annie."

The dog remained fixated on whatever had attracted her attention.

"Please, Sierra."

"He doesn't want to kill me. You, he'll dispose of. I'm the safest one out here."

She made a good point. Still, he wouldn't leave her. "Let's at least sit if you're insistent on staying out here and putting me in danger."

"That's mean." She rolled her eyes and marched back into the house.

Chuckling, Spencer followed. "Now, I feel better." He whistled for the dog. "Once I know you've locked up, I'll head home."

"Be careful." Worry shadowed her face as she locked the door when Annie returned to the house.

"I will." He gave her a quick kiss on the cheek. Shocked at his impulsive act, he rushed to his truck. So much for his resolve not to care for her in a romantic way. Seems his heart had other plans. Like he'd always said, he had a soft spot in his heart for anything hurting or in trouble.

With a heavy sigh, he turned the key in the ignition and headed up the mountain, wishing Sierra was going with him. At home, he put on his headlamp, then checked the perimeter of the clearing his cabin sat in.

No outside lights and a cloudy night plunged his home and yard into complete darkness. Not seeing anything out of the ordinary, he entered the house, lit an oil lamp, and filled Buster's food dish. "Sorry, boy. I've been gone too long lately. How about you go with me tomorrow?" He planned on being at the coffeeshop shortly before five to make sure Sierra got home unharmed. "Hopefully, you and Annie will become friends."

A hot shower later, he fed the fawn, then climbed in bed, his dog curled up at his feet. Why hadn't he been able to catch up to Dayton? The sedan seemed ordinary, not souped up. Since he hadn't heard from the police, it was safe to say they hadn't caught him either. The fact Annie had been wary of something in the woods confirmed that. He seriously doubted anyone else would be lurking around Sierra's place.

Instead of hanging with Sierra tomorrow night, he planned on staking out the woods behind her house to see if Dayton showed up. If he did, it would be the last time that crazy man got close to her. He eyed his handgun on the bedside table. Spencer would also be armed at all times from now on. If he'd had his gun, Dayton wouldn't have gotten away because he'd have been driving on three tires.

He grabbed his phone and sent Sierra a text: Goodnight.

She responded within seconds: Goodnight. Everything is good here.

Nice. He smiled and turned off the lantern on the table.

His window shattered.

A bullet slammed into the wall above his head.

Spencer grabbed his gun and rolled to the floor.

Chapter Seven

Shot at twice in one day was two times too many. Back plastered against the wall, Spencer kept his gun at the ready and peered out the window.

Buster's barking vibrated against his ear drums. "Quiet."

The dog's barks turned to growls. He kept his dark eyes on the window.

"Come on, Dayton. Show yourself." Spencer crawled from the bedroom, glass shards pricking his hands and knees. Once clear of the room, he got to his feet and slipped out the front door, quickly seeking shelter behind a bush. How had Dayton figured out where Spencer lived?

The chilly autumn night bit at his bare chest and toes. A breeze blew, adding to his discomfort and rattling tree branches that sported colorful leaves during the day.

Darting from bush to tree to outbuilding, he headed to where he thought the shot had come from. Buster stayed on his heels, emitting an occasional low woof in his throat. Fortunately, he'd trained the dog well. He wouldn't give them away.

At that moment, the clouds parted. The full moon

lit up the area like a football stadium.

Another shot rang out. Fire burned across Spencer's left bicep. He dove behind an oak tree.

"First blood." The voice came from a stand of aspen trees.

"Come on out." Spencer peered around the trunk, trying to catch a glimpse of the other man. "Face me."

"Stay away from Sierra. I know ways to get inside your head and drive you insane."

Spencer could play games, too. Instead of replying, he crept closer to where Dayton hid. No one else would care about Spencer being around Sierra. The other man had given away his identity.

"Find him, Buster." Spencer's voice rose barely above a whisper.

Nose to the ground, the dog darted off.

A crashing through the brush, signaled Dayton fleeing the other way. Spencer followed, the moonlight showing him the way. Blood dripped from the graze on his arm. Instead of chasing down a killer, he needed to be home tending to his wound. But that wouldn't protect Sierra.

He shoved a low hanging branch away from his face and stepped into the clearing of the hunter's cabin in time to see the flash of taillights speeding away. Dayton had been so close all this time.

Spencer marched back to his cabin and called the sheriff, then took a first aid kit from a shelf in the bathroom and cleaned his arm, pulling the skin together with butterfly band aids. Not as good as stitches, but would suffice.

After shrugging into a jacket, he fetched a sheet of plywood from his shed. He'd hammered the last nail in when Sheriff Westbrook arrived.

The sheriff approached and stared at the boarded-up window. "Good thing you weren't shot."

"I was." Spencer drew in a deep breath of crisp air. "Just a graze. Fixed it myself. Come on. I'll take you to the cabin."

"Can't we drive there?"

"Yes, but it'll take longer."

"I've got time. It's cold out here, and Karlie will have my hide if I get sick." He grinned. "She worries a lot since our own adventures in the spring. If she finds out you didn't seek medical attention, she'll badger you."

Most likely Sierra would, too. Spencer put Buster in the house, then slid into the passenger seat of the sheriff's car. "I think he's been staying in that hunter's cabin down the logging road to the east."

"I know the place. You sure it was Dayton Long who shot up your place?" The sheriff drove away from Spencer's.

"Who else would warn me away from Sierra?"

"True." He sighed. "I thought after the mess Karlie and I had gotten into because of her mother's secret, Misty Hollow was a quiet place again."

"Yeah, until a pretty gal brought trouble." Also because of a secret. Where could Dayton hide now? There were plenty of hunter cabins dotting the mountain, but how would he find them? Did the man follow roads until stumbling across one? That took too much luck to be believable.

The sheriff stopped the car in front of the now vacant cabin. "This is Fred Mason's cabin. It's been vacant since his death last year. His only child, a daughter, doesn't want it and plans on selling at some point. In the meantime, hunters stay here on occasion." He shoved his door open and stepped outside. "Hang back. I want to make sure no one is here."

"You could use the backup." Disregarding his orders, Spencer followed him into the cabin which looked much the same as the last time he'd been there. "He left his few belongings."

Sheriff Westbrook moved the sleeping bag with his foot. "I doubt he'll come back for them. Easier to purchase replacements."

"Which he'll buy in Lansing." A town thirty minutes away.

"Most likely." The sheriff returned to the porch. "I'll put out an APB. Maybe someone will spot him. He isn't going to leave town for long. Not until he gets what he wants."

Which was Spencer out of his way and Sierra in his clutches.

~

Stupid hick! Dayton punched his steering wheel, then tightened his grip when the car swerved toward the ditch. The man should be lying dead in the woods. How could Dayton have missed? He'd aimed for the man's heart.

Then that dog had come running. Why did people want the hairy things anyway? They smelled and shed, making a clean house impossible.

He drummed his fingers on the steering wheel. Where could he find a place to stay? No motel. The cops would look there first. What he needed was a computer and Wi-Fi. He could look up an aerial view of the mountain, scout out another cabin...no. Now that they knew he'd stayed in one, they'd look there, too. Still, it would take the longest for them to discover him.

The weather was too cold to live in his car. Not that he wanted to. He was better than that. He needed somewhere he could get warm. He'd figure it out in Lansing. One night in a motel wouldn't have the cops pounding on his door.

Tomorrow, he'd make a plan. One that resulted in a country boy's death and Dayton getting the woman he wanted.

His sister? Ha. He wouldn't feel this desire if she was blood related. His mother had lied! She'd given him away like an unwanted kitten. When he'd shown back up, she'd lied to keep him away.

~

Sierra woke refreshed the next morning. No alerts from the camera, and Annie had stayed right next to her on the bed. She let the dog out and fixed herself a bowl of cereal for breakfast. While she ate, she watched her dog wander the backyard.

Last night, Spencer had thought someone lurked in the woods out back. This morning, Annie didn't seem anxious. What kind of game was Dayton playing?

As a brilliant man, he had a plan, of that she was certain. She sighed and stepped away from the door. He'd try to grab her when she least expected it. Unfortunately for him, she wouldn't be taken easily and wouldn't go anywhere without her gun.

"See you later, Annie." Sierra locked her front door and headed for her bike. As she wheeled it to the front, she spotted Spencer in his truck. With a sigh, she took the bike back to the shed, then climbed into the truck. "You really don't have..." she narrowed her eyes. "You don't look as if you slept well."

"I didn't get much sleep." He looked as if he had something to tell her, but didn't want to. His gaze would land on her, then flick away.

"What are you not telling me?" She ran her gaze over him. "Why is there blood on your sleeve?"

"Dayton paid me a visit last night. A bullet grazed my arm. I'm fine. A little blood seeped through. No big deal." He drove the truck away from the curb.

"Did you go to the hospital?" A lump formed in her throat.

"No, I'm fine."

Dayton wanted Spencer out of the picture. That would leave Sierra alone and vulnerable. Still, that option was better than having Spencer dead. "I don't want you coming around anymore. Don't pick me up, don't check on me, nothing." She blinked back tears, the words cutting through her heart.

"Don't be ridiculous." He parked in front of the coffee shop.

"He's going to kill you."

"It won't be that easy." He turned to face her. "I'm not leaving you alone. The man is delusional. He's already killed someone, two if he's responsible for your mother's death."

"He's shot at you twice!" She yanked on the door handle, then shoved the door open. "I don't want him to succeed the next time."

"Have a little faith, Darlin'." He tossed her a wink. "See you this afternoon. I'm going to go get some sleep."

"You're infuriating." She slammed the door and, head high, stomped into the coffee shop.

"What bee got in your bobby sock?" Sue Ellen handed a man a coffee and shot a curious glance at the fuming Sierra.

"Spencer."

The other woman smiled. "Man trouble is the best kind."

"Not when they don't know where the boundary line is." She stashed her purse under the counter and sighed. She couldn't tell the other woman the exact problem with Spencer, so let her think what she wanted.

"Well, the fact that you're dating the hottest man in Misty Hollow must be some consolation."

If they were actually dating. Sierra pasted on a smile and turned to wait on the next customer in line. Thankfully, the shop was busy, and the morning passed quickly. When the time for her lunch break arrived, Sierra purchased a sandwich and tea and chose a table in the corner. She might be stubborn, but she wasn't stupid. Going for a walk, alone, on her break would be a foolish thing to do with Dayton on the loose.

While she ate, she stared out the window, wishing she'd brought a book to read. For a small town, quite a few people strolled Main Street. The small city was exactly the type of place she'd always thought she'd wind up living. Dayton ruined some of the beauty of the place. Would the attraction return when he was no longer around? She hoped so.

Bob, the mechanic working on her car, entered the shop. He glanced around, then approached her table when he spotted her. "Car's done." He dropped a set of keys on the table. "You can write me a check whenever."

"Thank you. I can do that right now." She retrieved

her checkbook from her purse, grateful to have her car back. She wrote the check and handed it to him. "I'll come by after work."

"No need. It's sitting in your driveway." He gave a nod and left.

That was a service she hadn't expected. Not that she really needed her car. She lived close enough to everything she needed that walking or the bike sufficed. She wadded up her napkin. But, then again, there was Dayton spoiling what she really wanted to do.

"Phone's for you, Sierra." Sue Ellen held out the phone Sierra hadn't heard ring. "Must be your man."

Why would Spencer call the shop and not her cell phone? "Hello?"

"I am your man, aren't I?"

Her blood chilled at the sound of Dayton's voice. "What do you want?"

"You know what I want. You also know I always get what I want. Tell your hick friend to stay away."

"I did. He's stubborn." She turned away from Sue Ellen's curious look. "We're only friends, though. You don't need to concern yourself." If she could convince him of that, maybe he'd spare Spencer.

"Anything that has to do with you concerns me."

"You're my brother."

"That's a lie!"

She closed her eyes, willing him to see reason. "I'm at work. You shouldn't call here."

"If you hadn't of changed your cell phone number, I wouldn't have to."

"I really have to go." The afternoon rush had started. "Goodbye."

"Get rid of him or I will." Click.

Sierra hung up the phone, her legs weak. How could she make Spencer go away before something bad happened?

"You have a brother?" Sue Ellen tilted her head. "I take it you two don't get along."

"You got it." Sierra pulled herself together and pasted on a smile. "I came here to get away from him." Keep as close to the truth as possible so as not to get caught in a lie.

"Some men are good at finding you when you don't want to be found."

Yes, and Dayton was one of those men.

DECEPTIVE PEACE

Chapter Eight

There'd been no sight of or calls from Dayton in three days. Sierra wasn't going to be fooled into a false sense of security, though. Her brother merely waited for the right time to strike. Spencer still drove her to and from work, but didn't hang around as much as he used to.

She couldn't fault him. He had his own life to live, his own things to deal with.

She nodded as a police car cruised past, then waved at Maggie, her neighbor. "Good morning."

"So far." The older woman's face wrinkled as she smiled. "I woke up so it's a good morning."

"I'll bring you a banana muffin when I get off work." Sierra pulled her coat tighter around her and headed to where Spencer's truck sat. "Hello."

"Hey." He smiled and drove away from her house. "Cold today."

"It sure is." She hated how stilted their conversations had become. But, she had no one to fault but herself. She'd done everything to keep him away short of a restraining order, yet the man persisted on driving her back and forth to work.

She cut him a sideways glance. If she were honest

with herself, she'd admit to missing his company in the evenings. With a sigh, she glanced out the window. When they stopped in front of the coffee shop, she couldn't get out of the truck fast enough.

"See you later." Spencer called out before driving away.

Heart heavy, Sierra entered the shop.

"Someone sent you flowers," Sue Ellen sang, motioning to a vase full of red roses.

Sierra knew before reading the card who they were from. Her hand trembled as she took the card from its holder and read, "For my woman, the other half of me." She crumbled the note and tossed it in the garbage. "Throw them out, please."

"From the wrong guy?"

"Absolutely. They're from my brother trying to right a wrong."

"That's kind of...creepy. Red roses from your brother." Sue Ellen shuddered.

Sierra stored her purse and donned her apron as the regular group of elderly gentlemen in overalls entered the shop. "Your usuals?"

"You know it," one called out. "We'll be at our table."

Sierra made four small coffees with room for cream and sugar, then carried them to the table. "Enjoy."

"Thanks, little lady." The man named Herbert frowned. "I heard someone had been squatting in Mason's old hunting lodge."

"I heard that, too." Another said. "Sheriff and Spence went looking, but the person was gone. Left behind some food and a sleeping bag."

Sierra's steps faltered. Spencer had told her Dayton had showed up at his place, but neglected to mention he'd been living that close to Spencer's cabin.

"Westbrook is scouring all the motels in the area. Seems like the squatter might be the man who shot Hank and tried to shoot Spence." Herbert shook his head. "You know anything about it, Sierra?"

"No more than you." She kept the smile on her face and returned to her place behind the counter. Dayton where are you holed up now? She glanced out the window, expecting him to be strolling down the sidewalk.

The hair prickled at the nape of her neck as if someone watched her. No one in the shop seemed to be paying her much attention other than placing their orders. She shrugged off the feeling. She wouldn't feel completely safe until Dayton was locked up.

On her lunch break, she took a sandwich from the selection the shop sold and sat at a table by the window. The sunny day looked deceptively warm, but the people huddled in their coats told the truth. A frigid wind blew.

She took a bite of her sandwich, then froze, the food tasting like cardboard as she swallowed. Dayton stood on the sidewalk opposite the shop and smiled at her through the window.

Relax. You're safe. He won't take you from a place filled with your new friends.

She tried tearing her gaze from his and failed. She barely blinked as fear choked her. After several tense minutes, he tossed her a wave and sauntered off. She set her uneaten sandwich down, appetite gone.

At the end of the day, Sue Ellen asked her to take out the garbage as she tallied the cash register. Sierra shrugged into her coat and stepped out the back into the alley. The wind from earlier had died down, but the late afternoon chill still seeped to her bones. She tossed the garbage, which included the roses, into the dumpster.

"Sierra."

Her mouth dried up. She slowly turned around. "Leave me alone, Dayton." She tried to step around him.

He blocked her path. "You will see the truth one day. Somehow, I'll make sure you do."

"Go away before I scream."

"Who will come? The barista? The shop is empty." He grinned. "I know your schedule, every step of your day. I know that in exactly three minutes, your hick friend will pull up out front to drive you home. I also know he hasn't been hanging around as much. That makes me feel better." He reached out to caress her face.

She ducked under his arm and burst into the shop, slamming the door behind her. After several deep breaths, she retrieved her purse from under the counter.

"You okay?" Sue Ellen glanced up.

"Freezing outside." Spotting Spencer's truck, she darted out of the shop and into the front seat.

He cut her a questioning look. "What's wrong?"

"Nothing." She forced the tension to leave her face. "Oh, I forgot Mabel's muffin."

"Want me to run in and get it?"

"Would you mind?"

"Not at all." He opened his door and jogged to the shop, returning seconds later with a white bag. "Sue Ellen had it waiting on the counter."

"Thanks."

At home, she dropped off the muffin at her neighbor's, then hurried home to feed and let Annie out. The dog didn't seem to like the cold any more than Sierra did and quickly wanted back in.

After a simple supper of soup and crackers, a comedy on TV she'd watched a hundred times, she climbed into bed, ready to forget the day. She'd just closed her eyes when the alert went off on her phone. She glanced at the screen to see Dayton approaching the house.

Sierra punched Spencer's number into her phone. "He's here."

~

"I'm coming. Hang up and call the police. You should have called them first." Spencer bolted from bed and grabbed a pair of jeans.

"I thought of you." Her voice wavered.

"Call now." He hung up and dressed as fast as he could. "Come, Buster." The big dog had chased the man away once, he could do it again.

His heart beat in his throat as he sped toward town, hoping, praying, he'd make it there before Dayton laid a finger on Sierra. She'd be okay. She had the dog and a gun. The man wouldn't be able to get close. He kept telling himself that all the way to her house.

Seeing a squad car out front, his shoulders relaxed. "Come, boy." He marched up the stairs and pounded on the front door.

A pale-faced Sierra opened. "There's an officer scouting the yard."

He pulled her into his arms. She trembled. "Let's sit. You're okay now." He led her to the sofa and kept an arm around her. "Tell me what happened."

64

"I'm sorry I bothered you." She took a shuddering breath. "Instinct, I guess. You did say to call if I needed anything."

"Yes, I did. Never apologize for calling me. I'm glad to be here." He really was.

"I'd just gone to bed when my alert went off. After I called you, I returned to that screen. Dayton walked around the perimeter of the house. He looked directly into the cameras and smiled." She glanced up, her tortured gaze wrenching at his heart. "He spoke to me at work today when I took out the garbage. Sent me roses."

Spencer's blood chilled. "He approached you?"

"Yes. He didn't try to harm me. Only told me he'd make sure I saw the truth someday. That he'd make sure of it."

He didn't like the sound of that. Was this part of the mind games he'd threatened? "I'm staying on your sofa tonight. Buster and Annie will keep us safe." He glanced to where the dogs nosed around each other.

The officer returned to the house. "No sign of the intruder, ma'am. Give us a call if he shows up again."

"I will."

"Stay put. I'll see the officer out and lock up the house." Spencer walked the policeman out. "I'll be staying here tonight, but would appreciate regular drive-bys."

"We've been doing that for weeks. First time the man has shown up here. We'll keep an eye out. I'll let the sheriff know that Long was spotted in town. Might be a good idea to put some motion lights and cameras a few feet into the woods out back. Give the lady a little more warning."

"I'll get on that tomorrow." Spencer locked the front and back doors and checked all the windows. By the time he'd finished, Sierra had placed a quilt and pillow on the sofa.

"You don't have to stay, but I appreciate it."

"Not a problem. You shouldn't be alone tonight."

She nodded and shuffled to her room, Annie right beside her.

Spencer stretched out on the sofa that was too short for him to fully stretch out and prepared for a night of not much sleep. Thank goodness his arm was healing nicely since it pressed against the back of the sofa. His right arm hung off the side when not on his chest. His feet hung over the armrest. Yep, it was going to be a long night.

He woke at dawn, stiff and sore. With a groan, he sat up and swung his legs off the sofa. If he spent another night, he'd sleep on the floor. Couldn't be worse.

"Mornin'." Sierra dragged her feet to the kitchen. "How'd you sleep?"

"Horrible. You need a new sofa."

"Came with the house." She pulled a can of coffee from the cupboard. "Want some?"

"Definitely." He stood and stretched, sighing as his back popped. "Today's your day off work, right?"

"Yes. I've some errands to run."

"Mind if I tag along? We could get lunch."

She shot him a narrow-eyed look. "I thought we talked about you not hanging around so Dayton doesn't target you."

He chuckled, crossing his arms. "I spent the night, Sierra. If he knows I did, the target on my back isn't going anywhere." And neither was he.

"Okay." Her shoulders slumped.

He stepped close behind her. "Is my company so bad?"

She turned, her face inches from his. "If it means danger to you, then yes. You're the first friend I made here. I care about you."

Friend? If they were in a different situation, could they be more than friends? Did he want to?

He stared into her eyes. Yeah, maybe he did.

~

The man had spent the night! So much for Sierra's vow they were only acquaintances.

Dayton punched a hole in the wall of the house he'd found. After several days of nosing around, he'd discovered they were in a warmer climate for the winter. He had a place to stay until March, at least.

Not that he'd need it. Sierra would be his long before then.

Maybe threatening the old woman who lived next door would convince Sierra of how serious he was. He wouldn't kill her unless he had to. Just send Sierra a little note of the consequences of spending time with Mr. Spencer Thorne. Oh, yes, he'd found out his name.

Knew all about him. Ex-military, served a term overseas, no family to speak of. Lived like a hermit until Sierra came to town. Respected within the community.

Dayton hated him and looked forward to ridding the world of Spencer Thorne.

Chapter Nine

Sierra sipped her coffee while Spencer made ham and cheese omelets. The man looked at ease in the kitchen. He should, she supposed, since he lived alone. Having him there, made her realize how loneliness after her mother's death lingered around her like a shroud.

"What kind of errands?" He set a plate in front of her.

"Groceries, post office, nothing major." The cheese oozed from the omelet. A long string hung from her fork as she lifted it to her mouth. "Mmm."

He laughed. "I enjoy cooking, even if just for myself."

"I might have you cook for me more." Her face warmed at the soft smile that graced his face. She cleared her throat and focused on breakfast. Her words sounded as if he'd be spending the night a lot more.

When she'd finished and put the dirty dishes in the dishwasher, she brushed her teeth and grabbed her purse. "Ready?" She glanced at Spencer lounging on her sofa.

"Yep." He snatched the keys to his truck off the coffee table. "I've some things to get today, too. The police suggested cameras a few yards into the woods and a house alarm to give you a bit more warning when Dayton comes along."

"I can't afford that. These other cameras already took too much of my savings." She locked the front door behind them.

"Consider it a loan. When this is all over, I'll take them down and put them up at my place."

She frowned. "As long as that plan is followed through with, I'm okay with the idea." As much warning as she could get regarding Dayton the better.

Spencer stopped at his truck. "Looks like we're taking your car."

She widened her eyes at the sight of four slashed tires. "So much for dogs warning us when someone comes around."

"The man is like a ghost." Spencer kicked one of the tires. "One more stop today. Make that two. I'll have to let the sheriff know."

"Here." She handed him her keys. "You can drive."

His mouth twisted. "Is that supposed to console me?"

Smiling, she shrugged. "Maybe. Is it working?"

"No." He laughed and pressed the fob to unlock the car doors. "Nice try, though." He slid into the driver's seat. "Mind if we get the tires and report the crime before shopping?"

"Not at all." She clicked her seatbelt into place as he drove the car around the truck, across her lawn, and off the sidewalk.

Spencer ordered four tires from Bob who promised to drop them off at the house later that day, then drove to the police station. While he reported the slashing of his tires, Sierra sat in a chair in front of the reception desk.

Being a small town, Misty Hollow didn't have the business a larger police station might have. The receptionist seemed bored as she blew on freshly painted nails. At least the town had been safe until Sierra led her brother there. She exhaled sharply. Things would return to normal when Dayton was stopped. Hopefully, that wouldn't be too far in the future.

Spencer returned with the sheriff, stopping in front of Sierra. "The sheriff thinks you should move to the cabin with me."

"Absolutely not." She hitched her chin. "I've security cameras at my place. We're closer to the police station. A secluded cabin on the mountain allows Dayton much easier access."

"Spencer said you'd say that." Sheriff Westbrook crossed his arms. "So, he'll be staying with you."

She opened her mouth to protest, but clamped it shut. The two men stood like bookends, forming a formidable opposition to any dispute she might make. "Fine." She stood and marched from the building.

When her and Spencer arrived at the car, she spun to face him. "No arguing, but you'll take the bed and I'll take the sofa."

"Nope. Too close to the front door. I've got a cot up at the cabin. I'll sleep in your room. If Dayton somehow manages to get into the house, I want him to have to come through me to get to you."

Which was exactly what she didn't want. Outnumbered by the men in her life, Sierra climbed back into the car. She couldn't fight them all. The sheriff and Spencer had her best interests at heart. She needed them to keep her out of Dayton's clutches. All she could do was pray no one got hurt.

"Don't be mad." Spencer reached over and gave her hand a squeeze.

"I feel as if I've been played. You really didn't expect me to agree to the cabin, did you?"

He gave a sheepish grin. "Guilty. I knew you'd say no. The plan was always for me to stay at your place. We'll have to go to Lansing to get the security cameras I'm wanting."

"Okay, sneaky man." She turned to stare out the window as they drove away from Misty Hollow.

She had no idea what life in the small town could be like. Her first night had been spent in a stranger's house. Then, she'd learned Dayton had tracked her to the town. Sure, she had her home, a job, and a dog, but life didn't have a feeling of normalcy. She'd come to Misty Hollow for a change of life after her mother's murder. The peace she thought she'd find there had been deceptive, and she had no idea what her future held.

~

It hadn't given him as much pleasure as he'd thought slashing the tires would. The warning hadn't stopped Thorne from spending time with Sierra.

When Dayton had seen the truck still there in the early hours of the morning, he'd reacted without thinking. Everything he did seemed to push Sierra closer to the man Dayton wanted out of the picture.

Now, he followed two car lengths behind, in a rented vehicle under an assumed name, as they drove down the Interstate. If the two were always together, how could Dayton get rid of Thorne without harming Sierra? Did he care? Obviously, she'd failed to see reason and made her choice.

The monster in his head confused him. He occasionally lost his sense of purpose, of who he was, of why Sierra didn't want him. Then, he'd remember the old woman's secret, her lies.

Anger burned through him. If he couldn't have Sierra, no one would. He increased his speed, passing the two vehicles in front of him and pulling in behind Sierra's car.

~

The ram from the car behind them whipped Spencer's head forward. His forehead hit the steering wheel, sending a sharp pain through his skull. "Tighten your seatbelt, Darlin'. We've got company." He pressed the accelerator, casting a quick look in the rearview.

"He'll run us off the road." Sierra turned to see behind them. "I thought he wouldn't harm me."

"Guess that changed." He whipped the car to the fast lane.

Horns blared as he sped past, followed by the silver sedan. Dayton's behavior was escalating fast. The only bright spot that Spencer could see was that it would all be over quicker. Hopefully, with him and Sierra still alive.

Another ram, this one harder, but Spencer had expected another hit and braced himself. He whipped the wheel to the right, slamming the other car when it pulled alongside them.

"He's going to kill someone!" Sierra gripped the hand strap above her head.

"Let's hope not." He glared at the stoic face of the

other man. Dead eyes. Stony expression. He didn't care if his actions resulted in someone's death. "I know a thing or two about evasive driving." He tore up the access ramp, through a red light, and down the exit ramp. A quick glance in the rearview mirror showed Dayton boxed in by cars at the stoplight.

Now was their chance. He continued driving above the speed limit for several miles before slowing just outside of Lansing.

"You okay?" He sent a quick look at Sierra.

"My heart is threatening to beat free, but otherwise, I'm fine." Her breath shuddered. "Let's get the things we need and get home."

"Won't argue with that." He sent another look behind them. "Uh-oh. He's back."

The silver sedan weaved in and out of traffic. He had to be going ninety miles an hour. Where had he ditched the black vehicle?

Spencer took the exit to Lansing, hoping to lose Dayton in the city traffic. If nothing else, they'd pay a visit to the police station. "Get out your gun, Sierra."

Her eyes rounded. "You want me to shoot at him?"

"That's a possibility." He turned right at a gas station. If they could get inside a store, they'd be safe. Dayton wouldn't try anything in a crowded place, would he? Sierra had told him about the man, but this behavior seemed over the top.

No available parking spots were available close to the electronics store. They'd have to walk and hope Dayton didn't run them over. Spencer pulled into a spot.

"Stay close." He took Sierra's hand once they exited the car, having her put her gun in the glove compartment. "If you see him, run for the store."

She nodded, eyes wide in a pale face. "I never thought he'd try to kill me."

"What did you think he wanted with you?"

"For me to be with him."

"Eventually, he'd realize that couldn't happen." He picked up his pace, pulling her along with him. "He may think he loves you, but his behavior borders more on hate." One more quick glance around the parking lot, and he opened the store door for Sierra, ushering her inside.

She stayed glued to his side as he filled a cart with the things he needed. Finished, they headed back to the car with no sign of Dayton.

"We should take a different route back to Misty Hollow," Sierra said. "My guess is he's waiting at the exit to the Interstate to catch sight of us. Dayton can be a very patient man."

"Smart thinking." He stashed his purchases in the trunk while she climbed back in the car. "Let's do all our shopping here in Lansing. Patient or not, he might get tired of waiting."

"He won't."

Two hours later, groceries purchased, and stamps bought, Spencer drove to the highway. It would add fifteen minutes to the drive, but they'd be able to see Dayton coming since there'd be less traffic. That was if he figured out they'd taken an alternate route.

No sight of Dayton on the drive back. Sierra's plan seemed to have worked. When they pulled into her driveway, four new tires were piled next to his truck.

IIc helped Sierra carry her groceries inside, then took the security equipment to the woods. "Watch my back, Buster. Don't let anyone sneak up on me."

When he'd finished that two hours later, he went to install an alarm on the house. "This is where you punch in the code to set the alarm, and again to disarm it. You'll have fifteen seconds to disarm after getting home before the alarm company is notified. They will call you. If they don't get an answer, they will then call the police."

Sierra watched with interest, biting into an apple. "Well, I guess I'm as safe in my house as I can be." She glanced at the big front window. "Unless he decides to break through the glass. He'd have us shot dead before the company was alerted."

"Nice thought." Still, he'd done all he could do. "I'll go get my cot."

Chapter Ten

As she'd thought, Sierra got little sleep with
Spencer just feet away. His soft breathing, the sounds
he made while he slumbered, all sounded loud in the
quiet of the night. Not to mention she'd lost her breath
when he'd entered the room wearing flannel pants and
no shirt. The man looked good, no doubt about it.

She glanced over at the cot, not surprised that he'd
awakened before her. She sniffed. Smelling coffee, she
tossed off the blankets and grabbed her robe from the
foot of the bed. Nothing got her up faster than the
aroma of brewing coffee.

For Pete's sake, man, put a shirt on. Spencer's
muscled back narrowed to a trim waist, his pajamas low
on his hips. He reached down and pulled them up
before resuming the cracking of eggs into a bowl.

Mercy. Sierra made a beeline for the coffeepot.

"Good morning." Spencer, oblivious to the effect
he had on her, smiled. "Sleep well?"

"Yep. You?" She poured a cup of coffee and added
a liberal amount of cream.

"Better than the sofa. Breakfast will be finished in
a bit. I'm making a quiche."

"You weren't kidding when you said—" An alert

on her phone cut her words off. "The camera in the woods has been triggered." She pulled up the camera on her screen as Spencer leaned over her shoulder.

Dayton strolled among the trees as if he had no worries in the world. At one point, he stopped and smiled into the camera. His lips moved.

"Is there a way to hear what he's saying?"

Spencer pointed to a microphone. "Push that to hear him, push this other one to speak back."

"So, we can listen in without talking back?" She pressed the button.

"Yesterday was fun, wasn't it, Sierra?" Dayton's brows rose. "I'd like to play some more games with you and Thorne. The cameras won't stop me. One night, you'll wake up to see me leaning over you. I'll find a way in. Ciao!" He turned and sprinted out of sight.

"Don't let him into your head." Spencer placed a hand on the top of her head, then returned to the stove.

"How can you not be concerned? The cameras don't faze him."

"Regardless of what he says, he can't get to you without going through two dogs and me. I know how to fight, Sierra. I know how to pull the trigger." The glance he sent her over her shoulder let her know he wouldn't hesitate if the time came. "Keep yours handy at all times."

She nodded. The gun sat on her nightstand within easy reach if she needed it during the night. But could she actually shoot a person? It would be far different than a target of aluminum cans.

Spencer slid the quiche into the oven. "I'm going to take a quick shower while that cooks. You going to be okay? I've already let the dogs out."

"I'll be fine." She stared into her coffee cup. Seconds later, the sound of the shower had her standing in front of the back door. What was wrong with Dayton that he'd be so obsessed with his half-sister? How could she convince him they had no future even if she wanted one with him, which she no longer did. She'd been pulling away from him for months before her mother's revelation. She'd been reluctant to announce an engagement, told him she wanted to wait a while, to get to know each other better, but he'd insisted.

Maybe it was time to look through her mother's papers. Maybe she'd find the answers to a few of her questions. She set her coffee on the table and marched to her bedroom, retrieving the metal box from the top shelf of the closet. Stomach fluttering, she returned to the kitchen.

"What's that?" Spencer looked up from his phone.

"My mother's papers. It's time I went through them."

A timer dinged, propelling Spencer from his chair. A few minutes later, he set a plate in front of her.

"Thanks." She opened the box to see a pile of envelopes. With a deep breath, she reached for the top one.

"The quiche is better eaten hot."

"Right." She set the envelope down, glad to procrastinate a few minutes more.

"Would you like to be alone when you go through that box? I can eat in the living room." Spencer reached across the table and put his hand over hers.

She drew comfort from his touch. "It'll be okay. I really didn't have time to mourn. At the funeral, Dayton started acting stranger than I'd ever seen him. Starting yelling and tried dragging me to the car. A couple of men got him off me. I rushed home, grabbed some things, and ran. That's the day I hit the deer and you found me."

"This will end, and you'll grieve. It's only a matter of time."

"I know. The quiche is delicious. Who taught you how to cook?"

His eyes softened. "My mother. Cancer took her five years ago."

"I'm sorry."

"You've never mentioned your father."

"That's because I don't know who he is." She exhaled heavily. "I loved my mother with all my heart, but she struggled to put food on the table, thus letting many men into her life. I came to terms with that a long time ago." She pushed her empty plate aside and reached for the envelope.

The first envelope contained last year's tax papers. The next one contained a will, leaving the house to Sierra and what little was in the bank account. Sierra didn't want the house. She'd rather sell it and buy a place in Misty Hollow. She was surprised at the ten thousand dollars in her mother's savings account, though.

At the bottom of the box, she found a birth certificate, some baby pictures, and a copy of adoption papers for Dayton. "I need to get these to my brother. If he sees this, it might sink in that my mother told us the truth."

"You can tell him the next time he triggers the cameras." Spencer turned from the sink where he rinsed the dishes before putting them in the dishwasher. "He's still wanted for murder. Hank's and your mother's if the authorities can prove he was responsible for her accident."

"Mom must have known the people who adopted him. Otherwise, how would she get a copy of the birth certificate?" She flipped through the photos. Dayton had been a cute kid. "I'd like to go talk to them. Maybe they can give me some insight into my brother."

"Had you met them before?"

"Yes. Once, after our engagement. I'm sure they were as shocked as I was to find out I'm their son's sister."

"We can go when you get off work."

"Don't you have a job?" She narrowed her eyes at him. "I've never asked what you do that gives you so much free time."

"My military retirement." He grinned. "I'm thirty and live off the land. I have everything I need."

"Don't you get bored?"

"Nah. There's plenty to do around my place. Now that you're here, I'm kept even busier."

Because of her, his place was being neglected. They needed to stop Dayton, and fast so both she and Spencer could get back to their lives. "It would still be best if you returned to your place so Dayton could see we aren't an item."

"That is not going to happen so stop bringing it up." A muscle ticked in his jaw. "This will be over soon, and I'll be out of your hair. Is it that awful that we're thrust together?"

Not in the slightest. "No. It's nice not to be alone when dealing with my brother."

~

Finally, Sierra saw reason about Spencer being around. Not only did he feel a need to protect her, but he realized how lonely his life had been before meeting her. He wished they'd met under different circumstances, though.

Spencer's hands clutched the steering wheel as they drove to Redford to visit the Longs. Would they answer Sierra's questions? Their son was a suspected murderer. How would they react after hearing that information?

"What if they won't talk to me?" Sierra asked softly.

"Why wouldn't they?"

"Embarrassment over the whole situation. I know I would be."

He frowned. "They had no idea who you were. Your mother may have kept up on the boy she gave away, but I doubt she shared information about you. She wouldn't have sent them pictures of you."

"True. She wouldn't have had a reason to." She returned to looking out the window.

Spencer continued to follow directions until they pulled in front of a small, cottage-style house on a few acres of land. "Here goes nothing."

"I hope it's something." She gave a shaky smile and opened her door.

Spencer followed her up the steps to a porch decorated will autumn décor. He reached around her to ring the doorbell, then stepped back.

A woman in her mid-sixties opened the door. Her eyes widened at the sight of Sierra. "I didn't expect to ever see you again."

"Do you mind if we come in? I have a few

questions about Dayton."

Her gaze flicked to Spencer. "Who are you?"

"Just a friend of Sierra's."

The woman's lips thinned. "Well, that was fast." She stepped back and ushered them inside.

"Just friends," he said again. If she thought he and Sierra were an item, she might not tell them anything.

She didn't look convinced, but told them to have a seat while she went to get her husband.

Spencer sat next to Sierra on a brown sofa covered with a colorful crocheted Afghan. "She doesn't seem very friendly."

"I should have come alone." Sierra sighed.

"Nope." He sat back, crossing his arms.

Mrs. Long returned a few minutes later with a man around her age who wiped greasy hands on a stained towel. "They'd like to ask questions about Dayton."

"Ain't seen him since his birth mother died."

"That's right. You were at the funeral." Sierra's eyes widened.

"Yeah. Sorry about how he treated you. Our son hasn't been well. He's been to the doctor a few times, but won't tell us what's wrong." He sat in an easy chair that matched the sofa and averted their eyes. "I'm starting to think it's something serious. Your mother's...revelation triggered something in him. He's not the same boy we raised."

"Mr. Long." Spencer leaned forward. "Dayton is a suspect in a murder. He's been stalking Sierra, making threats on her life. He's shot at me." As if reminding him, his arm burned where the bullet had grazed him.

Mrs. Long shook her head. "Our boy isn't capable of that kind of behavior. He's simply upset. He loved

Sierra."

"He's been changing for months," Sierra said. "Before my mother's secret."

Her husband gaze fell. "I'll be right back." He shuffled down a hallway.

The other three sat in uncomfortable silence. Spencer wanted to put his hands over Sierra's trembling ones, but restrained himself. The sharp gaze of Mrs. Long had him squirming as it was. He felt like a teenager under the watchful eye of a mother that didn't approve of him dating her daughter.

"Here. I found this in a file under his mattress." He handed Sierra a sheet of paper.

"Why were you looking there?" His wife asked.

"For something to tell us what has happened to our boy. He's always kept his secrets under his mattress since he was a little boy." His eyes filled with tears. "I wanted to spare you, since I doubted we'd ever see him again."

"A fatal brain tumor?" Sierra paled. "He was diagnosed last year. This is why he changed."

"Your son," Spencer said, "has become a very dangerous man. I suggest the two of you take caution."

"Why would he harm us?"

Spencer stood, pulling Sierra to her feet. "Because, as you said, he is not the same. He doesn't see reason, and he'll only get worse. If he thinks you've betrayed him in some way, he may come for you."

Chapter Eleven

They went to see his bogus parents? What did Sierra want with them? Had he removed everything from his room when he'd left?

Living with his parents at his age had been a bit unorthodox, but it had allowed him to save the bulk of his salary. Money he now needed to live on since he couldn't work with Sierra running wild. Of course, when he'd proposed to her, he'd started looking for the perfect house. Then, his mother lied and his whole world got upended.

Things were getting out of hand. He needed to move faster, do things on a larger scale. But first, he needed to find out what his so-called parents told Sierra and Thorne.

He waited until nine p.m. when he knew they'd both be in bed getting ready for a night of slumber, then pulled the key he'd kept from his pocket and unlocked the back door. Since they had no dog and no security system, he entered as silent as smoke. His gaze fell on white sheets of paper on the coffee table highlighted by the moon. His medical report. They knew about the monster in his head. Now, so did Sierra.

His right eye twitched as the pain in his head grew,

making it difficult to think. Come on. He pounded his head. Think. It's not as if he can march into their room and kill them. It needs to look like an accident.

Spotting the gas stove in the kitchen, he smiled. He stepped up to the stove and turned on the burner to light. How far did he need to be in order not to be blown up as well?

He moved to the laundry room and removed the line to the hot water heater before taking a candle from a box stashed in case of power outages. He lit the candle on the kitchen counter and sprinted from the house.

He was a mile away when the explosion happened. The fire ball reflected off his rearview mirror. Manic laughter burst from him. That had been fun.

~

The next morning, a bit more used to the sounds of having Spencer sleeping in her room, Sierra climbed out of bed rested. Again, the aroma of coffee greeted her as she entered the kitchen. Instead of standing at the stove, this morning, cup to his lips, Spencer stared at the small TV on the counter.

"What is it?" She stepped beside him.

"The Longs house blew up shortly after nine p.m. last night." He set his cup on the counter. "They suspect a gas leak."

"A bit coincidental after we paid them a visit." She sagged into a chair.

"I agree. Coffee?"

She nodded. "I work today. What will you do?"

"Work around my cabin after I drop you off. Then, I'll be there to pick you up at five."

Good. She hated that he neglected his place to look

after her. She pushed to her feet, poured herself a cup of coffee and turned up the volume on the TV.

"Since the Long home was set away off the road, no other homes were damaged in the explosion," the reporter said. "We believe the Longs were home at the time of the explosion. More details as we learn them."

Ill or not, Dayton was leaving a trail of death in his wake. When would it be Sierra's turn?

The alert sounded on her phone. She opened the screen. "Spencer."

Dayton motioned at the camera, his features hard. "Why would you go to the home of liars? What did you hope to accomplish?"

"Speak to him," Spencer said, staying out of sight.

Sierra pushed the proper button. "I know about the brain tumor, Dayton. Why won't you seek medical attention?"

"It would do no good. I only have a few months and wanted to spend them with you. You've made that impossible by rejecting me. If I can't have you, no one can. I will take you to the grave with me. You will be mine in the afterlife as you wouldn't while we lived." He scowled and marched back into the trees.

"He'll find a way." She shut off the app. "Somehow, someway, he'll get to me. I didn't have time to show him the birth certificate."

"Finding a way means going through me."

She nodded and met his gaze. "He's already come close. He shot at you twice and hit once. Next time you might not be so lucky."

"Which shows that whether I'm with you or alone, I'm a target." He put his hands on her shoulders, his gaze still locked with hers. "We're in this together."

"I've lost everyone. I don't want to lose you, too." Tears stung her eyes.

He leaned his forehead against hers. "You won't."

"Promise?"

He chuckled. "I promise."

A promise they both knew couldn't be guaranteed. "I'll get ready for work." She slipped free of his grasp and gathered her things for a shower.

One statement from her mother had brought a life Sierra enjoyed to its knees. Now, she ran from the very man she'd almost married. Surreal, unbelievable, and everything in-between.

The ride to the coffee shop was silent. Sierra got out of the truck, waving aside Spencer wanting to open the door for her. "There's no sense in getting out into the cold. I'll see you later." Steps heavy, she entered the coffee shop, knowing that at least there, surrounded by people, she'd be safe. But who would watch out for Spencer?

"Your brother still bothering you?" Sue Ellen measured coffee grounds.

"Yep." She caught a glimpse of a police car cruising down Main Street.

"You ought to sic the sheriff on him."

"They're looking." She donned her apron. "So far, he's evading them. Me and Spencer are the only ones catching sight of him. Turns out he's got a fatal brain tumor that's causing him to act this way."

"That makes sense, considering his obsession with you."

If she only knew. Sierra went to unlock the door and pasted on a smile as the first customers of the day entered.

~

Everything seemed the same as he'd left it when Spencer returned to his cabin. He took out the new window he'd purchased in town and leaned it against the wall before pulling down the sheet of plywood he'd nailed over the broken one.

Confident, Buster would alert him if anyone came around, he concentrated on his work and let his mind wander to the visit with the Longs. Dayton obviously needed help. Instead of trying to locate him, his father kept his son's medical condition from his wife. That seemed strange to Spencer. Now, they were dead, and there'd be no answers coming from them.

Dayton had only grown angrier when Sierra told him she knew of his condition. The insanity radiated from his eyes. If he wasn't stopped, he'd do something unimaginable and lots more people would get hurt.

Was there a way to stop him? If so, Spencer didn't know what it was.

He felt as if all they did was try to stay ahead of Dayton, instead of actually stopping him. He'd spoken into the cameras the last two days. Would that become a pattern? If so, Spencer could hide in the trees and confront him when he came to speak to Sierra again. Risky, but it might work.

When he'd finished replacing the window, he washed a load of clothes, tossed them in the dryer, and headed back to town to pick up Sierra. Halfway down the mountain, he realized a dark sedan hadn't turned off on any of the dirt roads branching off the main road. Not uncommon since the road he drove on was the only one leading to town, but the dented front bumper alerted him to the identity of the other driver.

Since Dayton only seemed to be following him, Spencer continued on his way. He wouldn't be any safer in town, the other man had shown that by shooting at him on Main Street, but if something did happen to him in town, there'd be witnesses.

He parked in the drugstore parking lot across from the coffee shop, choosing a spot that faced the street. Dayton slowed, tossed him a salute, then pulled into the parking lot of a bookstore which also gave a good view of where Sierra worked.

Spencer pulled out his phone and called the sheriff. "Long is in the parking lot of the bookstore."

"You're sure it's him?"

"Positive."

"What is he doing?"

"Taunting me and watching the coffee shop."

"Do not engage. I'm on my way." Click.

It didn't surprise Spencer that Dayton didn't stick around. He saluted again and sped out of town. Where was the man staying? He'd followed Spencer back to town. Did that mean he was holed up somewhere on the mountain or a motel on the other side? Spencer knew what he'd be doing while Sierra worked tomorrow.

She stepped out of the shop and glanced around. Spotting his truck, she stepped into the street and started across.

An engine revved.

Spencer watched in horror as Dayton sped toward Sierra. He'd never reach her in time, but shoved his door open anyway. "Sierra, run!"

Her eyes widened. She froze but a second before diving to the sidewalk.

Dayton sped past.

Spencer sprinted across the street as the sheriff turned around and gave chase to Dayton. "Sierra." He dropped to his knees beside her.

"I'm fine." She put a hand to her head, bringing it away bloody. "Guess I hit my head."

He smoothed the hair away from her face revealing a gash. "That's going to need stitches. Wait here while I get my truck." He hated leaving her, but with Dayton occupied at the moment felt she'd be safe enough.

Not caring that he blocked traffic, he parked in the road, then helped Sierra into his truck. He grabbed a napkin from the glove compartment. "Hold this against the cut. Are you nauseous? Seeing double?"

"A little nauseous." She rested her head against the seat. "I guess he really does want me dead."

"The sheriff chased him out of town. Let's pray he captured Long this time."

She nodded and closed her eyes, pressing the napkin against her forehead. "I'm ready for this to be over."

"You and me both, Darlin'." He waved a hand at the line of vehicles behind him and drove to Lansing, the closest hospital. Small towns did have their disadvantages. "Don't go to sleep."

"I'm not," she mumbled.

"Then open your eyes."

"The sun hurts."

He grabbed his sunglasses from his visor. "Put these on."

She complied, releasing a sigh. "That's better."

"Dayton parked for a while in the bookstore parking lot, then left. He must've been lying in wait for you to cross the street. From now on, I'll come inside to get you."

"Sue Ellen already doesn't let me take out the garbage."

"How much does she know?"

"Just that I have a crazy brother harassing me." She turned her head to face him. "I'm not sure how much of my story she believes, but she isn't asking a lot of questions."

"That's good. We don't want Dayton targeting her." If the sheriff catches up with him, they wouldn't have to worry about her brother anymore. He'd be locked up in a hospital until the tumor took him out.

It pained him to want Dayton to die, but he'd choose that man's death over Sierra's any day. He reached over and took her hand in his. She'd changed his life in a way he didn't think possible after returning home from his deployment. She made him want to be human again and not a hermit on the mountain.

On impulse, he lifted her hand to his lips and smiled.

Chapter Twelve

Sierra protested Spencer getting her a wheelchair. "I can walk. It's my head that hurts."

"You might be dizzy. Wait here." He jogged through the doors, returning with the chair.

She rolled her eyes and sat, secretly relieved. She did feel dizzy, and her head pounded with a ferocity she'd never experienced.

Fifteen minutes later, a nurse wheeled her into a curtained-off room. "Let's get you on the bed."

Spencer helped, then sat in a hard plastic chair while the nurse took her vitals.

"Doctor Reece will be in soon." She patted Sierra's shoulder. "You relax." She smiled at Spencer. "There's coffee near the nurse's station if you want some. Nothing more than ice chips for Miss Wells, though."

"I'm fine." Sierra pulled a blanket over her. Why were hospitals so cold?

The nurse cleaned the wound, then left them alone.

"Do you want some ice chips?" Worry creased Spencer's face.

"I'm fine. The doctor will stitch me up and send me home."

As if on cue, a doctor around Sierra's age slid past

the privacy curtain. "Hello, Miss Wells. You fell and hit your head?" He shined a flashlight in her eyes. "What's your pain from one to ten with ten being the worst?"

"An eight." She lied. The pain was almost unbearable. Especially with him shining a light in her eyes.

"Hmm." He clicked off the light. "You're suffering from a concussion. I'll have the nurse stitch up that gash while I write a prescription for pain meds. You'll be alright, but you'll need to take it easy for a few days."

"How long?"

"Three days." He smiled at her, then Spencer and left.

She groaned. Three days off work. She'd done nothing but hemorrhage money since arriving in Misty Hollow. Nor did she have medical insurance since she hadn't worked ninety days yet. Getting the funds from her mother's bank account and selling the house quickly became a priority.

The nurse returned, put three stitches in Sierra's forehead, then handed her a prescription. "Follow doctor's orders and you'll be right as rain in a few days. Call us if you get worse or have any questions. Stop at the front desk to pay your bill. God Bless."

"I'll make sure she does." Spencer stood. "Ready?"

"Yes." She sat up and held out a hand for Spencer to steady her as she got to her feet. Three hundred dollars later, she sat in his truck again and they headed to the pharmacy in Misty Hollow. Another twenty-five dollars later, they drove home.

Spencer's phone dinged. "It's a text. Can you look

at it?"

She read, then gasped. "The sheriff lost him. Dayton is still out there."

Spencer gritted his teeth. "I was really hoping it would end today."

She'd hoped so too. "Tomorrow, I need to go to my mother's bank and see a realtor. It's time to get rid of the house."

"Are you sure?" Spencer helped her from the truck and into the house. "The doctor said to rest."

"I need the money." She lowered herself slowly to the sofa. "There's been too many expenses in the short time I've been here." She hated saying it out loud. Hated admitting she needed her inheritance. All of this was Dayton's fault. She wanted to strangle him. She prayed he'd be caught and spend what little life he had left behind bars.

"I can give you a loan." Spencer sat beside her.

"Haven't you done enough already? A stranger arrives on your doorstep and uproots your life. That's more than enough." She regretted the bitterness lacing her words. Without Spencer, she might be in Dayton's clutches or dead. "I'm sorry. I'm tired, I guess."

"Let me make you some soup, then you can take a pain pill and go to bed." Spencer didn't seem daunted by her coldness. Instead, he did what he always did and rushed off to take care of her.

She never did anything nice to him. Oh, she'd tried to get him to go back to the mountain, the best thing she could do for him. Now, it was too late. Dayton already wanted both of them dead.

She watched as Spencer heated a can of soup on the stove. Why wasn't he married or at least in a relationship? Men like him didn't come along every day. Maybe she was meant to hit that deer. Maybe the only one who could protect her from her brother was Spencer. Her head hurt too much to think.

Pushing to her feet, she moved at a snail's pace to sit at the kitchen table. Spencer set a bowl of soup in front of her, some crackers, a glass of water, and a pain pill. "You'll make a good husband and father someday."

~

A father? Spencer never even contemplated marriage. Not even now as his feelings for Sierra grew. He had every intention of returning to his mountain life once Dayton was out of the picture. So said his head. His heart said something altogether different.

"I'll take care of the dogs now." What could he say to her remark? That a family wasn't in his future? He called to the dogs and opened the back door. While they sniffed and took care of business, he filled their food and water dishes.

Finished with their basic needs, he stared at the tree line. Where are you? He'd no longer wait until tomorrow to begin his search. He'd head out after Sierra went to bed. Annie and the security system would keep her safe, and he'd be back by morning.

By eight p.m. Sierra went to bed. Spencer waited until soft snores emanated from her, before grabbing his gun and Buster and set the alarm. The pain meds would keep Sierra sleeping for several hours. He called the police station from his truck and asked that a squad car park in front of her house.

"I don't think it's wise for you to head out alone," Westbrook said.

"He's on the mountain somewhere. He has to be. You've sent officers to every nearby hotel and found nothing."

The sheriff exhaled heavily. "Be careful and keep me posted. I did lose him up there. There're too many places for a car to pull off the main road. I'll send an officer to Miss Well's house."

"Thank you." Spencer hung up and headed for the mountain. There was one road that went up and over, but several dirt roads that led to hunting cabins and homes. He'd skip the homes since he knew they weren't empty and concentrate on the cabins. The mountain was as familiar to him as his own home. He'd find where Dayton holed up the same as he had before, and this time he'd be ready.

Buster sat in the front seat, his dark eyes focused on the road ahead of them. He might not be able to speak, but the dog was the best company Spencer had had before meeting Sierra. He reached over and ruffled the dog's fur. "You're still my buddy."

The dog whined and wagged his tail, thumping it on the seat. Having the dog with him, made Spencer feel less alone as he traveled the dark mountain roads in search of a maniac.

He drove up and down the roads for hours, finding hunter's cabin after hunter's cabin, with no sign of Dayton having stayed in any of them. There were more to check out, miles of dirt roads weaving around the mountain, but Spencer wanted to be back before Sierra woke.

He entered the dark house and turned off the alarm.

"Where have you been?" Sierra said from the sofa.

"You're up?" He turned on the light.

She sat with her knees drawn up to her chest and hugged a pillow. "Dayton was here again. The alarm woke me."

"The alarm?" His heart dropped to his knees.

"He rattled the back door handle, almost as if he were testing it. Spencer, he knew you weren't here. Annie started barking, the alarm was blaring, and you were gone."

"I'm so sorry." He sat next to her. "I went looking for him, trying to find out where he's holed up to on the mountain. I had no idea he'd come back here so soon." He pulled her head to his chest.

"As doped up on pain meds as I am, all I did after turning off the alarm was stare at my phone."

"What about the officer out front?"

"Oh." She blinked. "I forgot about him. Dayton came to the back door."

The officer should have heard the alarm. "I've got to go check on the officer. Lock yourself in the bathroom. There's no windows. I'll be right back." After making sure she actually entered the bathroom, he slipped out front. Glancing both ways, he approached the squad car.

"Officer?" A body slumped over the steering wheel. Spencer shook him, then checked for a pulse.

Steady. He checked for blood, finding a knot on the side of the officer's head. Knocked out, not dead. His racing heart returned to normal as he called Westbrook.

The sheriff mumbled, clearly having been woken.

"Sorry to wake you. This is Spencer. Someone attacked the officer outside Sierra's house. He's unconscious."

"Call an ambulance. I'll be there in ten minutes."

Spencer returned to the house and watched out the front window.

Chapter Thirteen

Sierra gave herself one full day to do nothing but rest her head. After that, she got up at six a.m., showered, dressed, and then marched to the kitchen to inform her handsome jailer that she needed to go to her mother's bank and house.

Spencer glanced up from something he read on his phone. "It hasn't been three days yet. Only half of that."

"I don't care." She poured herself a cup of coffee. "There are things I need to take care of. I feel fine." Other than a tiny headache, anyway. Nothing to keep her from doing what she needed to. "No arguments. I'm going."

He pressed his lips into a thin line. "I'll go get ready. Oh, and the officer attacked outside your house is going to be fine."

The officer was lucky. Dayton could have easily killed him. She guessed her brother didn't want a law enforcement officer's death added to his long list of crimes. While Spencer got ready, she returned to her room and the box her mother left her. She'd need the will in order to have the money transferred into her account and to put the house up for sale.

Sadness poured over her. She missed her mother so

much her heart had a permanent ache. Someday, she'd get the chance to grieve, to cry until her tears were spent, but today was not that day. She slipped the will into her purse and returned to the living room.

Spencer joined her five minutes later. "I want to know immediately if you start to feel bad. Don't lie. I'll be able to see it on your face."

Was she that readable? "Okay. We should take the dogs. It's a three-hour drive. We won't be back until late." She smiled and waited for him and the dogs to step outside first, then she set the alarm before following him to his truck.

"The bank will already be open when we get there," she said as they drove. "I'd like to go there first, then a realtor. I'll also have to hire someone to pack up my mother's things and store them until I figure out what to do with them. Do you think we can get that all done in one day?"

Spencer shot her a quick look. "If we don't dawdle. It'll definitely be late when we get home."

Home. She smiled and gazed out the window. He'd called her house home. A slip of the tongue, but still left her with a feeling of warmth and safety. She settled into her seat and kept watch through the side mirror for any sign of Dayton following them. The open road made them vulnerable. "We should have told the sheriff where we were headed."

"Good idea." Spencer grinned. "Why not give him a quick call. That way he won't think anything has happened when we don't return for a while."

She placed the call. The sheriff assured her they'd still keep a watch on the house and for her and Spencer to be careful. She assured him they would and hung up.

It felt nice for people to care about her, but she'd actually looked forward to starting a new life in Misty Hollow, relying on herself. How things had changed.

She studied Spencer's profile. Things had changed so much she couldn't imagine him not in her life. She sighed. He'd return to the mountain once Dayton was stopped. It was just as well. Then, her life would return to a new normal.

"What?" He arched a brow.

"Nothing." She smiled and resumed looking out the window. She must have dozed off, because when she woke, Spencer was pulling into a spot in the bank parking lot.

Squaring her shoulders, Sierra clutched her purse and marched into the bank and asked to see the manager about closing an account and transferring funds. Spencer preferred waiting in the front, leaving her to tend to her business alone.

"Have a seat, please, Miss Wells." The manager, a trim, balding man waved her into a seat. "You wish to transfer the funds from your mother's account into yours?"

"I have the death certificate and the will." She fished the items from her purse. "I've moved, so it's more convenient for me to transfer."

He glanced over the forms. "Everything seems to be in order. Would you like us to issue you a check or a wire transfer?"

"If you can wire transfer, that would be best." She wouldn't have to worry about losing the check while running around town.

"The funds will be there in three days. My condolences on your loss."

"Thank you." She stood and shook his hand. "I'm going to list the house for sale. It's better if I make a clean break."

"I understand. Here is a realtor I've used in the past." After handing her a business card, he walked her back to the front, nodded at Spencer, and then returned to his office.

"That was easy." She smiled up at Spencer. "Let's hope the listing of the house is the same."

He placed his hand on the small of her back, sending an electric current through her. The feel of his touch had grown too familiar to her. She pulled away, trying not to dwell on the puzzled look on his face.

She should never have allowed her emotions free reign. It would only lead to heartbreak.

"Let's grab lunch after meeting with the realtor." Spencer held the bank door open for her. "I'm starving."

She laughed. "You're always hungry."

He shrugged. "How far is the realtor office?"

"Right around the corner. We can walk. Will the dogs be okay in the truck?"

"Yes. It's cool enough." He hit the truck fob to make sure the doors were locked.

The real estate agent, a pretty middle-aged woman in slacks and a sweater was more than happy to agree to meet them at the house in an hour. "Hello, I'm Lauren. Yes, I know the property you're talking about. I've driven by the house plenty of times. It's a lovely little place. We'll have no trouble selling it."

"Do you have someone you can recommend to pack up the house's contents and store them?"

"Yes, we can handle that for you. Where did you

relocate?"

"Misty Hollow."

The woman frowned. "I've never heard of it."

"It's a small town in the Ozarks. See you later."

Outside, she glanced up at Spencer. "I guess our sleepy little town really is out of the way."

"That's what I like about it."

~

"Look around," Spencer said. "People everywhere. You can smell the car exhaust in the air. The noise assaults my ears. No, give me a sleepy little town any day."

"You're right. I'd never noticed it before."

He hadn't missed the way she'd pulled away from his touch earlier. She didn't seem bothered by his company, but she'd never reacted that way before. It surprised him as to how much her action had hurt. He liked touching her, feeling the warmth of her body, even in small ways. Her light flickered through the darkness of a loneliness he hadn't known he felt.

"You know this town. Where can we eat outside with the dogs?"

Her forehead wrinkled. "I know a pizza place with outdoor seating. I don't think anywhere will let the dogs sit with us, but they'll be able to see us."

"Then, it won't matter. It's too cold anyway." He shoved his hands in his pockets and marched to the truck, surlier than he'd felt in a long time.

They chose to sit inside out of the chilly autumn day.

"Does your mom's house have a yard? The dogs will need to go out." He slid into one side of a vinyl booth, leaving the other for Sierra.

"Yes, and it's fenced. Did I say something to upset you?" She crossed her arms. "You act as if you've a bee in your shorts."

He grabbed a menu from the end of the table. "I'm fine."

"Seriously?" She pulled the menu from his face. "Talk to me, Spencer."

He exhaled heavily. "I'm just tired. The cot isn't very comfortable."

"Then I'll buy another bed and you can sleep in the other bedroom. It won't take but a minute to clear it out."

He'd seen the room she used for storage. It would take a lot longer than a minute. "Once I eat, I'll be just fine." Hunger always made him act like a bear. "Really." And he would. He'd apologize, stop acting as if he and Sierra had a future, and continue on in the same way until Dayton was caught. Then, he'd return to his hermit ways.

Unfortunately, that didn't have the same lure it once had. "The fawn is growing. I'm sure it'll join some other deer soon."

She arched a brow and glanced down at her menu. "That's good." After a couple of minutes she asked, "Want to share a pizza? The mega meat sounds good."

"That's perfect." He closed his menu and returned it to its spot. When the waitress arrived, he ordered a large mega meat thin crust and a couple of sodas. There'd be some left over to sneak the dogs a slice each.

"Do you still think Dayton is hiding on the mountain?" Sierra sipped her diet soda.

"He has to be. The police have checked every

motel and hotel in a twenty-mile radius." He straightened against the back of the booth. "I don't see him going very far from where you are."

"Not until he kills me anyway."

"Murder/suicide." The thought made him ill. "He doesn't want anyone else to have you, and I don't believe he wants to live without you."

She paled. Her hand trembled as she set her soda glass down. "I think you're right. He won't shoot me from a distance. He'll want to watch as I die. I don't think he would've run me over the other day. That was nothing more than a warning." Her tortured gaze clashed with his. "You're in his way. He'll get rid of you first."

"As I said before, I won't be that easy to kill." He started to reach over and place his hand over hers, but stopped and pulled back.

"What if he hides in wait? Shoots you from far off?"

"Then he does. What do you want me to do?" He frowned.

"Not die," she said softly.

This time he didn't stop from taking her hand. "I'll do my best."

He didn't release her hand until the server arrived with their pizza. He didn't speak again until he'd eaten two slices. Feeling like a human again, he said, "Let's not worry about Dayton today. You've still got the realtor to see. I'm sure there are a few items from the house you'd like to take with us today. There's room in the back of the truck."

"You're right." She wiped her mouth with a napkin, drawing attention to her lips. They seemed so soft. Just made for kissing.

He gave a silent groan and focused on eating. Maybe food hadn't been the only thing he was hungry for.

He had the server box up the last few slices, then returned to the truck and made two dogs very happy. He laughed as the pizza disappeared in the blink of an eye. "Way to taste the treat, you two."

"Is that good for them" Sierra tilted her head.

"It doesn't hurt once in a while. They won't get to eat for a long time yet." Still grinning, he got in the driver's seat. "We'll have time to let the dogs out before the realtor arrives."

~

When would they realize they couldn't escape him? Dayton had watched from the bank, then across the street as the two enjoyed a pizza together.

He'd thought about doing away with the dogs while he had a chance, but he liked animals. They were more honest than people. The dogs couldn't help who their owners were.

Now, he sat in his car a few houses down from where the lying witch had lived. Where Sierra had grown up. What were they doing?

His question was answered when an SUV with a realtor sign on the door pulled into the driveway and parked next to Thorne's truck. Time to sell the old place. If it was because of money, all Sierra had to do was come to him. He'd leave her everything if only she would spend his last days at his side.

She might, too, if not for the country bumpkin. He cupped his hands around his head. "No. She made her choice." And it wasn't Dayton. "Sierra must die, too," he whispered.

As the realtor made her way to the front door, his mind devised a plan. One that would finish Sierra and Thorne off once and for all.

Chapter Fourteen

Tears pricked Sierra's eyes. Her mother had been so proud of the little two-story Victorian. She'd saved for years to buy the fixer-upper. Now, back to its former beauty, there'd be no family member to enjoy the place.

While Spencer kept an eye on the dogs, she climbed the stairs to the bedroom she'd spent half her childhood in. The same frilly pink and white bedspread with matching curtains. Her collection of Nancy Drew books. Very little had changed since she'd left. She picked up the well-loved stuffed bunny from her bed and carried it to the window.

She smiled at the trellis still nailed to the outside wall. More times than she could count she'd snuck out, using the trellis as a ladder. A red convertible approached the house. With a sigh, Sierra returned the bunny to its place on the bed and returned downstairs to greet Lauren.

"Gorgeous." Lauren smiled as she stepped into the foyer. "Your mother did a good job restoring this old house. It will sell very quickly. Why don't you want it?"

"I prefer small town life." Sierra ran her hand over

the banister. Her fingers picked up the dust. "I guess once the house is packed up, a cleaning crew will need to come in."

"That will be done before the house is staged." Lauren toured the house, then laid a contract on the kitchen table. "Look this over and return it to me. Then, we'll get the ball rolling."

"I'll bring it by before we leave town." Sierra walked her to the door.

"Then, I'll wait in my car. No need to come back to the office if you'll have it ready that quickly."

Sierra smiled and closed the door. "I thought I was ready. Now, I'm not sure."

"There's no rush." Spencer's calm gaze settled on her. "The house isn't going anywhere."

She plopped onto a kitchen chair. "It's time to make a clean start. I only want a few things from the house. What do I do with the rest?"

"Auction, unseen, the contents of a storage pod. All gone in one sweep."

She laughed. "You think of everything. Can you get the dogs? I want to sign this contract and get it to Lauren."

"Sure thing."

Sierra scanned the contract, then signed her signature. Time to let go. She turned the knob on the front door. The door wouldn't budge. "Spencer? The door is stuck."

"So is the back door." He joined her. "The dogs are fit to be tied outside." He yanked a set of curtains open.

Flames licked the frames, devouring everything in its path. Burning too fast.

Sierra's heart leaped to her throat. "Dayton is

burning the house down with us in it. Can you see Lauren?"

Spencer stood on his tip-toes to see over the fire. "I don't think she's alive. I'm not positive, but I think her throat has been slashed. We need to get upstairs. The fire department should be here soon." He pulled his phone from his pocket.

Smoke seeped around the door like greedy fingers. "There's no cell phone service way out here. No neighbor closer than a mile." She couldn't hear over her pounding heart and the crackling flames. "Break a window."

"The entire perimeter of the house is engulfed." He grabbed her hands. "Is there an attic? Someone will see the smoke and investigate. We need to get as far away from the fire as possible."

"Yes." They'd burn. The flames were growing. Soon they'd reach the roof. "We're going to die here."

"No, we aren't." He pulled her up the stairs after him. "The attic, Sierra?"

"Here." She led him down the hall to a door.

One glance down the stairs filled her with dread. She gasped, then coughed. Smoke was filling the first floor at an alarming rate.

"Come on." Spencer held the door open. "Find something to stuff under the door. It might buy us some time from smoke inhalation."

True, but once the fire reached them, the floor would collapse, and they'd fall to a fiery death. She opened the first trunk she came to and pulled out a wool blanket. "Here."

Spencer shoved it against the bottom of the door.

Sierra opened the round attic window and leaned

out. The flames hadn't reached her bedroom yet. It seemed to her as if Dayton had focused on the front porch and the back deck. A gas can lay on its side under a massive magnolia tree. "We might be able to climb out. Will that trellis hold your weight?"

"We'll have to jump over the fire. Can you do it?"

"I'll risk a broken leg rather than burn."

"That's my girl." He leaned backward out the window. "I'll need to climb up first, then pull you up."

Her foolish heart had leaped at being called his girl. Silly when she knew it was a mere slip of the tongue. "Okay. Be careful." She shot a quick glance at the door, relieved no smoke crept in. Maybe they would survive the day.

"Well, you won't have to worry about selling," He said, right before his legs disappeared out the window.

"Not funny." She leaned out and glanced up.

He reached down. "Grab my wrist."

She eyed the burning rose bush on the ground. "Don't you dare, drop me."

~

"I wouldn't dream of it." Spencer lay on his belly and stretched his arm as far as he could. "Sit on the windowsill, then slowly get to your feet. The sill is wide enough to stand on and hold onto."

Eyes wide in a pale face, she nodded before hopping up to sit.

"Not to rush you, Darlin', but the longer this takes, the bigger the fire under us." He gave her what he hoped was an encouraging smile.

"Okay." Gripping the sill on both sides of her, she got to her feet and reached up. "I can't reach."

"It's only an inch or two. You'll have to jump. I'll

catch you." Please, God, let him catch her.

"Are you crazy?!" She shook her head. "I'll wait for that someone to come you said would notice the smoke."

"I lied. No one is coming. Now jump or we'll die." He hated his curt tone, but now was not the time to succumb to fear. The sound of the fire grew louder. They were running out of time.

"I'm coming." She jumped.

His fingers wrapped around her wrist. Her's clutched his. Inch-by-inch, he scooted backward, scraping his skin on the roof shingles. For such a little thing, her weight worked against them. "Grab the roof."

Her free hand flailed, finally gripping the gutter. Spencer crawled forward, now taking both her hands in his and pulling her the rest of the way up before laying back for a few seconds to catch his breath.

"Now what?" She peered down at him.

"I've been thinking about that trellis." He got to his feet and stared over the edge of the roof. "It's long enough to reach the magnolia tree. If I can get it loose from the house, prop one end on the bedroom window frame and the other on the tree, we can crawl across it like a ladder."

"You do realize there's at least five feet from where we are to the window, right?" She narrowed her eyes. "How do you expect to get down there?"

"Same way we got up. Climb."

"The trellis that is burning is my childhood window. Dayton knew that." She put a hand on his arm and pointed. "We'll have to use the one by my mother's room. I've never tested that one. I don't know how strong it is."

He glanced toward the road. No one came to their aide. "We don't have a choice." By the time anyone noticed the smoke, the roof would be gone and them with it.

He moved carefully on the sloped roof, keeping one hand firmly around Sierra's wrist. They'd come too far for her to fall now. His heart would shatter if something happened to her.

On the edge of the roof where the second trellis still stood, he released her. "Don't move." He lowered to his belly and reached down to grip the top of the trellis. Nailed firmly to the building. He needed something to pry it away from the side of the house.

No other way. He'd have to lower himself to the trellis and ripped it away while climbing on it. He turned around and hung his legs over the edge.

"What are you doing?" Sierra reached for him.

"Getting you out of here."

"You'll fall."

Probably. But, if he didn't get the trellis to form a bridge, or come up with another plan, Sierra was stuck on the roof. He locked gazes with her and let go.

He gripped the trellis.

His weight pulled it away from the wall. While the fall went quickly, it felt as if he floated in slow motion. The snap when the nails and other holdings released sounded over the fire.

Sierra screamed.

The trellis stopped ripping away.

He dangled in mid-air. Glancing down, he noticed only three feet between him and the ground. He released his iron grip and cupped his hands around his mouth. "Stay there. I'm going to look for a ladder."

Idiot. Where else could she go?

From the attic window, he spotted a small garden shed behind the house. He hopped the fence, dodged eager dogs, and sprinted for the building. Bingo. A foldable twenty-four-foot ladder leaned against the far wall. He lugged it back, grateful the ladder was aluminum and not wood. Sierra would be lucky not to get burned as it was.

He leaned the ladder against a section of the wall that seemed to burn with less ferocity as other parts, but the fire was growing in intensity. He didn't like how extended it was, but if he placed it closer to the side of the house, she'd never escape getting burned. "Hurry, Sierra."

Sirens wailed in the distance. Better late than never.

She backed off the roof, pausing when she caught sight of the flames licking at the ladder.

"Don't stop. You cannot stop. Not even if you get burned. I'm waiting for you." His heart pounded as she scurried down the ladder. Once free, she launched herself into his arms.

He cupped her face. "Are you alright?"

"Yes. I burned my hands, but not badly." She released a shuddering breath. "Now that we're down, I'm really upset about my Nancy Drew collection." She smiled up at him.

Throwing caution to the wind, he lowered his head and claimed her lips with his. He'd never been more frightened in his life and put every bit of his emotion into the kiss until they were both breathless. Coming up for air, he leaned his forehead against hers. "The paramedics will care for your hands," he whispered.

She wrapped her arms around his waist and leaned against his chest. "Shut up and hold me."

Chapter Fifteen

Sierra sat inside the door of the ambulance while a paramedic tended to her hands. Her gaze fell on the burned ruins of her mother's house and Lauren's body on the lawn. The setting sun cast long shadows over it all. The realtor's throat had, indeed, been slashed. Dayton left her in the driver's seat to bleed out and most likely watch as he poured gasoline along the perimeter of the house.

Made to watch as she bled out with no chance to cry out an alarm. Determination to bring Dayton down increased. He'd taken the house and the memories, he'd killed again, almost adding Sierra and Spencer to his death toll. No more. The time to end this was long overdue.

In order to catch Dayton, Spencer would have to give her some space. He needed to get close to Sierra. If Spencer wasn't there when Dayton confronted her, he might not kill her right away. The authorities would have time to save her. She prayed so anyway.

"The burns weren't too bad. You were lucky." The paramedic smiled. "Sorry about the house. It was a beauty."

"Thank you." She hopped out of the ambulance

and glanced around for Spencer. He wouldn't like her plan, but would have to go along or she'd leave town. Something she didn't want to do.

She found him speaking with the local police and fire chief. "Do you have a minute?"

"Sure. Excuse me." He followed her away from the others. "Your hands okay?"

"They're fine." She stared into the face she'd grown to care so much for. "You saved my life. I would have never gotten out of the house without you."

"If I wasn't in the picture, you would never have been in the danger you are. Dayton no longer wants you with him. Now, he's willing to kill you."

"That's what I want to talk to you about." She took a deep breath and squared her shoulders.

"I'm not leaving you."

"I understand that. What I'm proposing is that you stop taking me to and from work. Dayton needs to approach me. Even take me with him. You can track me by my phone. It's our best chance of preventing him from killing anyone else and catching him."

His brow lowered. "It's too dangerous."

"I'm pretty sure that if he takes me alone, with you nowhere around, he won't kill me. At least not right away. He wants me to spend what little time with him he has left."

"As his wife." He crossed his arms.

"I can deflect him easily enough."

"Not if he overpowers you."

True, but she refused to be swayed. "It's the only way. People are dying, Spencer."

"And I don't want you to be one of them." His shoulders slumped. "Let's talk more when we get home, okay? We're both exhausted."

That she could agree with. "Are we free to go?"

"Yes. There's nothing we can do, and the detectives will contact us if they need something. Same with the fire department. It's obvious the fire was set. You shouldn't have a problem with your mother's insurance company." He placed a hand on the small of her back and guided her toward her car.

This time she didn't pull away. How many more times would she get to feel his touch? Once her brother was caught, he'd have no reason to come around. He'd return to his peaceful life on the mountain.

She dozed on the way home. There, she took a quick shower to rid her of the smell of smoke, then climbed in bed while Spencer took her place in the shower. She fell asleep, remembering his kiss, before he finished.

The aroma of frying bacon woke her. How did he do it? He'd had as difficult a day yesterday as she had, yet he still woke up before her. She glanced at the clock. Eight a.m. She'd slept ten hours and was late for work.

She quickly dressed in black slacks and a long-sleeved sweater. Grabbing her purse, she darted from the room. "Gotta go."

"I've already told work you would be late." He set a plate of bacon and eggs on the table. "When I explained why, Sue Ellen was very understanding."

"You really are a gem." She sat, getting a very good taste over the last few weeks of how life will be for whatever lucky woman manages to snag Spencer as her husband. Envy flooded through her. Kind, caring, strong, brave, excellent cook...bossy. She chuckled and dug into her breakfast.

He sat across from her. "I've been thinking about what you said yesterday.

Her hand holding a strip of bacon paused halfway to her mouth. "And?"

"I think we should speak to the sheriff before you go to work. You can walk to work from there."

"So, you agree not to take me back and forth?"

"Unless the sheriff believes otherwise, yes. I thought long and hard on what you said, and I see the merit in it. Dayton does need to be stopped."

Her phone beeped. "The camera." She opened the screen and reached for her mother's box she'd set on the table the night before.

Dayton stood there holding the wreath that once hung on Maggie's door. An icy fist gripped Sierra's heart. She pressed the microphone. "You had better not have hurt her."

"Not yet, anyway." He gave a cold smile. "But it would be easy, Sierra. Remember that." He tossed the wreath into the trees.

"You burned my mother's house down." She fumbled in the box for his birth certificate.

"Focus, Sierra," Spencer said softly. "Don't antagonize him."

She nodded. "Listen to me, Dayton, please."

His stare pierced the camera.

"This paper is your birth certificate. It lists the same woman as your mother that mine does." Oh, please listen to reason. "We are brother and sister."

"She brainwashed you." He practically spit the words. "Anyone can make a fake birth certificate."

"It has an official seal." He wasn't listening. She

wouldn't change his mind.

"I see you have bandages on your hands." His features softened. "I'm sorry you were hurt."

"You tried to burn the house down with me in it." She'd decided to leave Spencer out of any conversation with her brother.

"You made me angry. Don't make me angry again." He turned and marched into the woods.

~

A birth certificate? For a brief second his mind considered the fact Sierra might be right. Then, the monster in his head convinced him what a lie she'd said.

Dayton didn't care. She'd see things his way soon enough. Already, a plan formed in his mind. One that couldn't fail.

If only the hick had been in the house alone yesterday. He'd have stayed and watched for a while. As it was, he couldn't bear to watch the house burn with Sierra inside.

How had they escaped? The mountain man seemed stronger than Dayton had given him credit for. It would have taken a lot of strength and adrenaline to escape the house. He kicked at a rock in his path, sending it rolling into a pile of dry leaves and wished he could do the same with Thorne's head.

No matter. Sierra would belong to Dayton soon enough and the hick would be left with nothing.

~

Sheriff Westbrook listened without speaking until Spencer finished telling him of what had transpired the day before and what Sierra wanted to do about it. He quirked his mouth. "The two of you were very lucky.

Since he's killed again and threatened Miss Maggie, I don't see we have any choice but to lead him to believe he'll get what he wants." He folded his hands on the top of his desk. "It will be very dangerous, Miss Wells."

"I can't have more people die because of me. My brother is deeply troubled. Having him think I might be turning around to his way of thinking will save lives. Once he has me, you and your men can save me."

"Your brother may die in the process."

"He's dying anyway." She clutched Spencer's hand. "It might be best to die by gunfire than the slow and painful death he has waiting for him."

She was right. Spencer wouldn't want to die by a brain tumor. He'd rather his death be quick. "No more officers outside her house. The cameras will suffice." He swallowed against the lump in his throat as fear threatened to consume him. "I won't be staying with her anymore, either."

"That's not going to work." The sheriff straightened. "Park your truck somewhere and sneak in. Miss Wells should be safe enough riding her bike to and from work, but staying alone at night doesn't sit well with me."

Spencer glanced at Sierra. "I can sneak in."

"Okay." Resignation settled over her face. "You arrive after dark and leave before dawn."

His heart settled a bit. He could still protect her. What he wanted to do was lock her in a tower somewhere no one could get to her.

One of the hardest things he'd ever had to do was let her walk out of the police station and head to work without him. Spencer got into his truck wanting to follow her, but knowing he'd be spotted by Dayton if he did. There'd be no more parking across the street to wait for her to get off work.

Instead, he'd spend his days trying to locate where Dayton holed up. The proverbial needle in a haystack so far. While everything in him wanted to follow Sierra, he turned the truck toward home. "You ready to spend more time away from Annie?" He reached over and petted Buster's head. "Yeah, me neither."

He stopped at his cabin first and tossed his dirty laundry in the hamper. He hadn't seen the fawn in a few days. The little guy must have found a group of his own kind. At least Spencer hoped a predator hadn't gotten him.

He surveyed the stack of firewood outside. He'd need more before winter really set in. He could take care of that chore before driving aimlessly around the mountain. Grabbing the axe from its hook on the outside cabin wall, he whistled for Buster and headed into the woods.

A cold wind kicked up. Spencer stopped and leaned the axe against a tree before zipping up his jacket. Once he started chopping he'd warm up, but right now the frigid air ripped through him.

Buster didn't seem to mind. Nose to the ground, he went this way and that along the well-beaten game trail. Spencer smiled and headed to where he'd seen a dead tree just off the path. Hard work would help keep his mind off what might happen to Sierra.

Worrying wouldn't add an extra minute to her life and would only give him an ulcer. She'd be careful. She had a gun and knew how to use the weapon. Everything would be fine. If he told himself that enough, he might come to believe the words.

Buster barked ahead of him. Not the type of bark that came from treeing an animal. This bark came as a warning.

Gripping the axe, Spencer increased his pace, wishing he'd brought his gun along. With a full freezer, he hadn't the need for more meat and had left it behind like an idiot whose mind was occupied on something other than what he was doing.

"If that's you, Long, come out and face me."

No response other than birds blasting from the trees.

"Buster." Spencer put two fingers to his lips and blew a shrill whistle. When the dog didn't return, he broke into a run.

He should've suspected the thick leaves on the trail hid something. If he hadn't been worried about his dog, he might have. He planted his foot squarely in the middle of the pile. Iron teeth bit into his ankle. With a sharp groan, he hit the dirt.

Chapter Sixteen

Take that. "How's it feel, Country Boy?" Dayton watched through the trees as the man fell. The dog already slept from the drugged treat he'd given it. The dog would be fine in a few hours. His owner not so much. Help was a long way away.

Dayton could waltz up and finish the man off, but the slow death of spending winter on the ground, held in place by a bear trap would be far more satisfying. Maybe a predator would find him and all that would be discovered would be the bones of his foot still in the trap.

No one would know he'd done the deed. Hunters stepped in traps. It'd look like an accident. If Sierra did care for Thorne, she'd turn to Dayton in her grief.

All his plans were falling into place. Shoving his hands into his pockets, he strolled back to his car, whistling a lively tune.

~

Sierra spent more time glancing out the window for sight of Dayton than she did pouring coffee. Her distraction didn't go unnoticed by customers or her boss.

"Do you need to take the day off?" Sue Ellen

125

asked. "The bandages on your hands make you clumsy, and you seem worlds away. The customers are commenting."

"I'm sorry." Sierra took off the headset she wore to take drive up orders. "I'll just run the register if that's okay. I can do that easily enough." Her hands did hurt, and she'd wrapped just enough bandage around them to keep them clean, but she'd go crazy sitting at home. She needed to be out and about if her plan was going to work.

A police car cruised slowly past. She narrowed her eyes. If Dayton caught sight of a police officer, he'd never make a move to take her. Excusing herself, she moved to the back of the shop and called the sheriff.

"Why is there a police car driving up Main Street?"

"Because they've always done that a few times a day, Miss Wells."

"Oh. Sorry."

"Is this getting to be too much for you? We can put you in protective custody somewhere Mr. Long can't find you."

"That would only prolong things. I'm sorry for overreacting. Goodbye." She hung up and leaned her head against the wall. Idiot. Of course, the authorities patrolled town. Deviating from their regular routine would alert Dayton that something was up.

She glanced at the clock. Ten a.m. Only two hours had passed. How would she get through the day?

By lunchtime, she'd become a mess of nerves. Her head pounded. Maybe her idea to lure Dayton out of hiding hadn't been a good one. If it went on for a few days, she'd lose her mind. It would be her that needed to be hospitalized.

"Take an hour for lunch," Sue Ellen said, frowning. "You're driving me crazy. Anxiety radiates off you. Go somewhere for a bit. Go buy a silly romance novel to take your mind off things."

"Good idea." She purchased a sandwich and bottle of water and headed down the street to the bookstore. As she walked, she kept a close eye on her surroundings, expecting to see Dayton watching her. Why wasn't he? She usually spotted him at least once a day.

The fact he wasn't doing his usual worried her more than him stalking her. After another long look around, she pushed open the door to the bookshop. It had been way too long since she'd bought a book.

Once, she used to curl up each evening and read. Things had changed since coming to Misty Hollow. Sue Ellen was right. A good book would occupy her mind.

"Hello." A young woman smiled from behind the desk. "New to town?"

"About a month. I'm looking for a sweet romance. Something to take my mind off a stressful day."

"Follow me." Still smiling, she led Sierra to a rack of books. "You're sure to find something you'd enjoy. Give me a holler if you need anything."

After half an hour of browsing, Sierra carried three books to the counter. "Is there somewhere I can sit and eat my sandwich while I read?"

"The coffeeshop?" She rang up her purchases.

"I just came from there, Thank you." She could choose a table in the corner. It wasn't exactly what Sue Ellen had advised, but it would suffice.

After thirty minutes reading about a fictional

character's struggle with love and dating, Sierra was ready to finish out her workday. The next few hours passed without the nervous energy of the morning. At five o'clock, she put on her coat, grabbed her purse and bag of books and told Sue Ellen she'd see her tomorrow.

She resumed glancing over her shoulder as she strolled home, thankful that tomorrow she'd have her bike since Spencer wouldn't be driving her to town. Strange how much she missed seeing him waiting outside the coffee shop for her.

Safely at home, she let Annie out, filled her food dish, and heated a can of soup for herself. Simple and satisfying on what promised to be a very cold night. She sat at the table and read while she ate. When she'd finished, she curled up on the sofa to read until Spencer showed up a little after dark.

When dark fell and he didn't arrive, she put the book down and pulled up the security app on her phone. Everything looked clear. No sign of Dayton. He always showed up by now to communicate with her through the camera.

She got up and went to stare out the back door. Not seeing anything, she moved to the front window. Still nothing. Dread skittered down her spine like an icy finger. Where were the two men in her life?

Her mind whirled with the worst possibilities. A shootout with both of them lying injured. A fatal accident on the road. Something kept them away. She snatched her phone from the table and sent Spencer a text asking him when he planned on coming. When he didn't respond within fifteen minutes, she called him.

The call went straight to voicemail.

"Spencer, where are you? I'm getting worried. There's been no sign of Dayton today, and no word from you. Call me." She hung up, her palms beginning to sweat.

Something was terribly wrong. She dialed the sheriff's number.

~

Spencer woke to a whining Buster licking his face. Immediately, the pain in his ankle left him breathless. Had he actually passed out? He struggled to a sitting position and peered through the darkness to evaluate the damage.

Steel teeth clamped around his ankle. While the worse pain he'd ever experienced, he didn't think the bone was broken. He needed something to pry it open.

He tried using his fingers, but they trembled too much to be effective. Nausea rolled in his stomach. Cold seeped into his bones. Thankfully, the trap kept him from bleeding too badly. That would all change once he got free, and he'd need to get home fast.

What kind of idiot put a bear trap in the middle of a path? He froze, remembering the taunt from Dayton. Spencer's dash through the woods after his dog. No one ever died from a trap. What had he thought would happen? Hypothermia? Wild animal food? Both of which could happen if Spencer didn't get home.

He glanced around, his gaze settling on the axe. It might work at prying the trap open as long as he didn't cut off his foot doing so. He stretched for the axe, his fingers curling around the handle.

Taking a deep breath, he shoved the head between the trap's teeth. He yelled as the trap parted, but didn't stop until it lay fully open. He fell onto his back to catch his breath. When his head stopped spinning, he got to one foot and started the long, painful hobble to his cabin.

He had to stop way too much and lean against a tree. Buster would look up at him and whine, clearly wanting to be at the cabin. Which would need a fire lit. He patted his pockets for his phone, then remembered he'd plugged it in to charge so it would be ready when he went to Sierra's. She must be worried sick about him.

He picked up the pace the best he could. His shoulders relaxed as the cabin came into sight. A man stepped around the corner, freezing Spencer in place. Running was out of the question.

The man sprinted toward him. As he came closer, the moon revealed the face of the sheriff. "You alright? Miss Wells phoned me that you hadn't arrived and weren't returning her calls."

"Stepped in a bear trap."

"Let me help you." He shoved his shoulder under Spencer's arm. "Once we get inside, you call Miss Wells while I get a fire going and take a look at your ankle. You feel frozen despite your coat."

"It's a bitter night." Bless you, Sierra. He would've barely made it home on his own.

"You should really lock your door," the sheriff said, pushing the cabin door open.

"Until Dayton I never had a reason to." He closed his eyes in relief as the sheriff helped him into a chair.

"Sit tight." Sheriff Westbrook hunkered in front of the fire and stacked kindling before lighting with a match. A couple of logs later, he returned to Spencer. "Let me look at your ankle. I'll be very surprised if you don't need to go to the hospital."

"Let me call, Sierra." He punched her number into his phone.

"I've been so scared, Spencer."

"Like a fool, I stepped into a bear trap. I don't know how long I lay there, and I can't thank you enough for calling the sheriff."

"My heart told me something was wrong."

"I'm glad you listened." He hissed as the sheriff rolled up the leg of his jeans. "Let me call you later, okay? I'll be there, I just don't know when."

"As long as you're safe, I don't care. Get yourself taken care of. I'll see you tomorrow night. Everything is fine here."

"Are you sure?"

The sheriff glanced up. "I'll have someone drive by regularly. If Long was going to make a move, he would have already. Your high-top boots helped protect you some, but I strongly advise a trip to the hospital. The skin is mangled pretty good. This is bound to get infected if you don't."

Especially since he lay there for several hours after the accident. "I'm not going to argue." He allowed the sheriff to help him up and to the car out front where he stretched out in the backseat.

"Why do you think Dayton hasn't made contact with Sierra?" He grimaced as he adjusted his leg.

"I don't know, but I don't think it's good."

"I think he set the trap. I thought I heard him speak to me after I fell, but can't be certain. Buster was barking, then he stopped. I ran after him without looking where I placed my feet. It's a good thing I didn't fall on my axe."

"Might not have hurt as much." Sheriff Westbrook grinned in the rearview mirror, then sobered. "It could have been a lot worse. Let's not worry about why Long didn't make an appearance today. The man is ill. He could by lying down somewhere waiting for a killer headache to subside."

Or making a devious plan. That's where Spencer would place his bet. He leaned his head back and closed his eyes, trying not to focus on his ankle.

If Dayton had set the trap, why hadn't he come back and finished Spencer off? He'd been helpless. If he'd really thought lying out there would do the job, he underestimated Spencer. He'd never stop fighting to keep Sierra safe until he drew his last breath.

Chapter Seventeen

Sierra had worried about Spencer all night and wanted to call him before she left for work, but hesitated. Being wounded, he'd need his sleep. She sighed and dropped her phone in her purse, hoping he'd call when he woke.

"See you later." She patted Annie on the head, set the alarm, and locked the door behind her. Since the weather had grown so cold so fast, she kept her bicycle chained to the front porch. She eyed the car in the driveway. Why freeze?

She drove the car to work. The heater didn't have time to really get to work, but it kept her out of the wind. She found a parking spot not too far from the shop. A gust of wind accompanied her inside the coffee shop as she opened the door.

"Brrr." Sue Ellen glanced up. "No bandages today?"

"No. My palms are red and still a little tender, but not bad. I'll put ointment on them and wrap them when I go to bed tonight. It's too hard to do anything with them wrapped." She stashed her purse under the counter and grabbed her apron. She'd no sooner tied the strings than the regulars started arriving. "Good morning, Gentlemen."

"Good to see you doing so well, Sierra," one said. "I'll take my small black with room for cream and sugar."

"Of course." She smiled and took his order, then the next, calling them out to Sue Ellen. If the store got any busier, they'd need more help.

Soon, every table was full as folks wanted to take a break from running errands and get out of the cold. Sierra grinned. "This must warm your heart."

"It does." Sue Ellen nodded. "Opening a business in a small town is always a gamble. I'm happy this one paid off. Oooh, who is this hottie?"

Sierra's grin faded as Dayton, dressed in jeans, a button up shirt, and a navy blazer entered the store. The clothes reminded her of what he'd worn the first time she'd met him. "My brother."

"He doesn't look so bad."

"Don't let his looks fool you." Her eyes widened as he locked the door behind him, then started lowering all the blinds.

"Hey, Dude. I'm working and need that light," a patron said.

Dayton pulled a handgun from his pocket and aimed it at the young man. "I don't think you need the light now, do you?"

The man shook his head and closed his laptop. "I'm done."

"What are you doing?" Ignoring the pain in her hands, Sierra gripped the counter.

"I figured this was the best way to get you to listen to me." He smiled. "Seems I have to take you captive, along with a few others in order to get you to listen."

"I'm listening." God, help them all.

"Let's have a seat, shall we?" He glanced at Sue Ellen. "Coffee is on me." Then he looked around the shop. "Everyone stays in their seat. Don't make me use this." He set the gun on the table. "Sit down, Sierra. I'm sure one of the local yahoos have alerted the police by now. We don't have much time."

She lowered herself into the chair he pointed to. "Do you want something to drink while we talk?"

"You know what I like."

"A tall, iced coffee, Sue Ellen, please."

"Make it a hot one," Dayton said. "It's cold today."

Sierra folded her trembling hands on the tabletop. "So talk."

"One second." He took up the gun and turned as the young man he'd spoken to earlier tried slipping out the back door. "Foolish me. I forgot that door." He raised the weapon and fired.

The young man's back arched, then he fell with a cry. A woman screamed.

"I told everyone to stay in their seat." Dayton shook his head and moved to lock the back door. "Let's try again."

Red and blue lights flashed through the window blinds.

"That didn't take long." He exhaled as if the whole thing was nothing more than a nuisance and returned to the table where Sierra sat.

"You didn't have to kill him." Tears stung her eyes. "It's me you want."

"Now, you're beginning to understand." He sat across from her, his back to the wall so he could see the entire place. "I really thought you'd have some compassion after hearing about my health."

"I do feel for you, Dayton. Really, I do, but as a sister. You want something I cannot give you."

"I want your undying devotion!" His face darkened. "You loved me as a future husband once, before all the lies."

"They aren't lies."

"Stop." He slammed his hand on the table, making her jump.

The phone rang. Seconds later, Sue Ellen said, "It's for you, Mr. Long?"

"Tell them I don't have time. I'll talk to the sheriff later." He leaned on the table, his dark gaze locked on Sierra's face. "Are you frightened?"

"Yes." She squared her shoulders, willing the trembling in her limbs to stop. "You aren't well. The tumor has turned you into a monster."

The blow came too fast for her to duck and knocked her out of her chair. One of the men at a nearby table stood to come to her aid, only to be stopped when Dayton aimed his gun at him.

"I'm okay." She put up a hand and climbed back into her chair. "Please, no one leave your seat on my account." Her jaw ached, and she'd bit her tongue. The metallic taste of blood filled her mouth.

When Sue Ellen brought Dayton's coffee, she also brought a bag of ice wrapped in a towel. "For your face." She glared at Dayton, setting his cup hard onto the table.

"Ah, your friend doesn't like me much."

"I don't waste time on men who abuse women." She snarled and returned to the counter.

"Men wouldn't have to if women would keep their

place."

This wasn't the Dayton she had once thought she wanted to marry. The Dayton she'd first met had been kind, funny, and courteous. This new Dayton was evil and mean.

"We'll both leave this place in a few minutes," he said. "I'll take you to where I'm staying. In the morning, we'll flee the state and get married. Think of how rich you'll be when I die. Isn't that worth a couple of months with me?"

"You. Are. My. Brother. I have the birth certificate in my purse. If you let me—"

"So you can get your gun?" His mouth quirked. "Oh, yes. I've followed you from day one. I know exactly what is in your purse."

The phone rang again. Dayton cursed and marched to the counter. "This is Dayton Long. I presume I'm speaking with Sheriff Westbrook. What do I want? Isn't that obvious? I want Sierra Wells. Here's what will happen. Her and I will leave this place unhindered, or I will start shooting the hostages. Is that understood?"

~

"You can't let them leave together." When Spencer had gotten the news that Dayton held the coffee shop and all inside hostage, he'd rushed to town, fearing the worse. He now stood with the sheriff, his gaze never leaving the front door of the shop. "You need officers at the back door."

"Already there. I can do my job, Spencer. Long hung up, saying he'd give me a few minutes to think over his offer." He faced Spencer. "We have no choice. I can't risk the lives of everyone else. You've said he doesn't want to hurt Miss Wells."

"He's unstable." Spencer leaned heavily on the crutch he used. "No one can be certain what he'll do to her."

The blinds on one of the windows shifted, then fell back into place. The sheriff's phone rang. "He wants to talk to you." He handed the phone to Spencer.

"Let her go," Spencer growled. "If you hurt her…"

"Why would I do that, Thorne? My question to you is why won't you die?"

Anger roiled in Spencer like a tsunami. "I don't like making things easy for people like you."

"Keep him talking," the sheriff said. "We're going to try and get the back door open."

"People like me? What kind is that? We aren't so different, you and me. We're both willing to do anything for the woman we love."

Like a punch to the gut, Spencer realized Dayton was right. He'd do anything for Sierra, even kill. The only difference is that one of them was insane and the other determined. "What you want isn't possible."

"I wish everyone would stop saying that. Anything is possible, Thorne. Absolutely anything. Want an education, go to school. Want a job, write a resume. Want someone gone, kill them. Want a woman, take her."

Spencer could feel the man spiraling downward during their conversation. "Let me talk to—"

"Ah, sneaky. My apologies, Thorne, but I must go answer the back door. Tell the sheriff to call off his men or someone dies in three seconds. Once…"

"Call them off, sheriff!"

"Two…"

"Now."

"Three..." A gunshot sounded a mere breath before the two officers around back returned to the front.

The phone in Spencer's hand vibrated. "Yeah."

"Now, two people are dead because nobody wants to follow orders. I am bringing Sierra out. As much as I don't want to, if anyone tries to stop us, I will kill her. Am I making myself clear?"

"Crystal." Spencer sagged against the car. "I'll have the sheriff pull everyone back. Do you need a vehicle?"

"I'll take hers." He hung up.

Spencer handed the phone back to the sheriff. "They're coming out. He wants you to pull your men back."

"Fall back!" The sheriff waved his hand as the front door to the shop opened.

Dayton stepped out, Sierra in front of him. One arm snaked around her waist. The other hand held a gun to her head.

Spencer's heart lodged in his throat as the two moved slowly down the sidewalk toward Sierra's car. Dayton's cold gaze clashed with his. His lips curled into a smile. The man thought he'd won. The fight wasn't over yet. Spencer still breathed, and still stood, even if only on one leg.

Sierra's wide eyes implored him not to make a move. "I'll be okay," she mouthed.

He nodded, unable to respond back or Dayton would see. Surely, she knew he'd move heaven and earth to find her. His shoulders sagged. She didn't have her purse. There was no way to track her. "We'll never find her."

"As long as his phone is on, we will." Sheriff Westbrook grinned. "I've already got someone on finding out his number. We'll find out where he's taking Miss Wells."

Dayton was too smart for that. He'd ditch his phone at the first opportunity.

The man opened the passenger side door for Sierra. She slid across into the driver's seat, leaving the passenger side for him, effectively keeping herself between the polices' guns and Dayton.

With one more glance at Spencer, she started the car and pulled away from the curb. Those inside the coffee shop started pouring out.

Spencer hobbled after the sheriff and into the shop where a young man lay dead at the back door and a woman bled profusely from a shot to her side. Her eyelids fluttered. "This one is still alive."

"Thank God." Sheriff Westbrook knelt beside her, pressing napkins against the wound. "Get someone to call for an ambulance."

"He wanted me to give you this." Sue Ellen held out a phone. "Said it's his, and there would be no more communication coming from him."

Spencer's heart dropped to his feet. His gaze met the sheriff's. "She's gone from us."

"We'll find her. They'll be on the mountain somewhere. I'll call for reinforcements."

Spencer nodded and hobbled outside to stare in the direction they'd gone. They had headed for the mountain, some of which he'd already searched. With help and a map, they'd complete the search. He prayed they'd find Dayton's hideout in time.

Chapter Eighteen

Sierra took one last glance in her rearview mirror to where Spencer leaned on his crutch in the middle of the road. Then, she turned a corner and lost sight of him. Please don't let it be the last time she saw him. She blinked back tears. She'd have to stay focused and be ready to escape when the opportunity presented itself.

"Where are we going?" Her voice shook. She cleared her throat in an order to shove her fear down into the pit of her stomach.

"I've a place on the mountain for tonight. Tomorrow, we head west, then south. I like the weather in Mexico."

"I don't have my passport, Dayton. I lost it, remember?" Her hands tightened on the steering wheel.

He opened the glove compartment and pulled out her passport. "It's been here. Something told me we'd need it." He grinned, tapping the gun against his temple. "I'm always thinking ahead."

What else did he have planned? At least he didn't seem to want to kill her. She'd be dead already if that was the case. Stopping Spencer coming over, at least as far as Dayton knew, had to be why she still lived.

Although she hated him for trying to burn down the house with her in it.

"You're awfully quiet," Dayton said.

"You killed people." She narrowed her eyes, refusing to look at him. "Brain tumor or not, what you've done is wrong."

"That wasn't me. Surely you understand that." He put a hand on her arm. "There's something inside me. Something evil I can't control."

He was serious. Somehow, he'd removed himself from his actions. "If that's true, then put the gun down and we'll head back. You can turn yourself in and get the help you need."

"Shut up!" Spittle flew from his mouth. "You're with me now."

She shrank away from him. Obviously, questioning him or pointing out what he should do wouldn't keep her safe. "I'm sorry."

"Good. Don't speak unless asked." He set the gun in his lap. "Turn left."

Following his instructions, she headed up the mountain. A few miles up, they passed where she'd hit the deer her first night on Misty Mountain. Would this place also be where she spent her last night?

"I have a surprise for you," Dayton whispered.

His statement sent a trickle of fear down her spine. She usually liked surprises, but could guarantee this one would be different.

"Turn right."

She turned, wishing she could leave a trail of breadcrumbs for the sheriff's department to follow. Another left, then left again down a path that no one could call a road.

Tree branches, mostly devoid of autumn foliage now, scratched the sides of the door like skeletal fingers. Sierra shivered, wishing Dayton had given her time to grab her coat. He'd raced her out of the coffee shop as if afraid the sheriff would storm the place. Maybe he would have, given time.

"We're here." Dayton shoved open his door.

Here was a dilapidated shack that a strong wind would blow down. "How in the world did you find this place?"

He laughed. "By going off the beaten path. It isn't pretty, but it has sufficed. No one will find us here. We're safe."

She was anything but safe. She slammed her car door in the hopes someone was close enough to hear. All it accomplished was to startle some birds out of a tree.

Spencer knew this mountain. He'd lead the sheriff to her. All she had to do was hold on until then and find a way to escape if possible.

"Let's go." Dayton led her into the shack and motioned to a new sleeping bag. "That isn't your surprise though." He grinned, sliding a tattered curtain away from one of the windows.

Sierra's mouth fell open. Her blood turned to ice. Hanging on the wall was the yellow dress and straw hat she'd worn on their first date. A picnic near a lake in the city park. "How?"

"Imagine my surprise when I went through your mother's house after her death and found this hanging in your closet. Seeing that you'd kept these things confirmed the fact we are meant for each other. Why else would you save them?" He tilted his head.

"I left a lot of things behind, Dayton." She'd have been more than happy to continue believing anything she'd kept from her days with him had burned with the house. "Things I planned on donating." Until he'd killed her mother and sent Sierra on the run.

"There are so many things I've done for you." He leaned against the wall. "You have no idea."

"You've killed people. I know that." She crossed her arms and glared. "Was our mother the first?"

"Your mother! Not mine. All lies." He shook his head vehemently. "Stop spreading lies. Change your clothes."

"That's a summer dress. I'm already freezing."

"Change. Your. Clothes." He spit each word. The hard glint in his eyes alerted her that she'd pushed him to the edge of violence.

"Where?"

"Here." He grinned. "Don't worry. I won't ravish you. I'm waiting until we're married."

Thank God for small favors. Her shivers increased as she disrobed. The thin fabric held the bitter bite of winter as it slid over her skin. She removed the ponytail holder from her hair, letting the strands fall past her shoulders, then set the hat on her head. "Can I at least wrap up in the sleeping bag?"

"In a minute." Tears filled his eyes. "Let me look at you. Just for a moment. You are so beautiful, Sierra."

Once, those words had filled her with warmth. Now, they had the opposite effect. She stood awkwardly, like a shy teenage girl waiting to be asked to dance. Shivers overtook her and she grabbed the sleeping bag, wrapping it around her shoulders.

Dayton sighed. "Oh, well. Mexico will be

warmer."

Sierra dropped to the floor in a corner and wrapped the sleeping bag tighter around her. The shack sported so many holes in the wall, the cold wind whistled through the cracks. She kept a wary eye on Dayton, waiting for him to let down his guard.

"Get some sleep, Sierra." Dayton rolled up in his bag. "We leave at daylight."

~

Spencer hated the crutch that kept him from pacing. He wanted to go looking for Sierra now. The sheriff wanted to gather a search party. He saw the reasoning in the plan, but everything in him wanted to head up that mountain and save Sierra.

Sue Ellen offered him a cup of hot coffee. "Trust the sheriff. He knows what he's doing."

"Thanks." He took a sip of the drink. "I know, but it's hard. Dayton Long is unhinged. There's no telling what he'll do to her."

"He's had plenty of opportunities to harm her and hasn't."

"He tried to burn down the house she was in."

"Only because you were there. He has her to himself. Have faith." She patted his arm and moved to hand someone else coffee.

"Head out in five minutes," Sheriff Westbrook said. "I want every single road on that mountain searched. If you find them, radio in. Do not make contact with Dayton Long. Remember, he is armed and dangerous."

Spencer checked the gun on his hip. Dayton wasn't the only dangerous man in Misty Hollow.

"Spence, you're riding with me." The sheriff

marched toward his car.

"Why can't I go alone?" He hobbled after him.

"Because I don't want you going off half-cocked." The sheriff met his gaze over the top of the car. "Your heart is in this more than your head."

The man was right. Spencer's mind was clouded with pain and fear. He needed to be with someone level-headed. He took a deep breath, drawing on his military experience to build that shield he erected when emotions needed to be squelched. He gave a definitive nod and opened the back door for Annie and Buster to jump in before getting into the passenger seat.

"I've already searched this side of the mountain," he said, clicking on his seatbelt. "It might be a better use of our time to search the other side."

"Are you sure you didn't miss anything?"

"Positive. I even checked game trails."

"Then, I'll take your word for it." He sped out of town. While the other searchers branched off the main road over the mountain, the sheriff continued to follow, finally pulling over. "We walk from here. Let's see if the dogs pick anything up. Can you manage?"

A car pulled up behind them and a pretty red-haired woman with a black German Shepherd exited. "I thought you could use some help."

"Spencer, this is my wife, Karlie. She's no stranger to danger." He gave her a quick kiss.

"Nice to meet you, ma'am. Don't worry about me. Nothing's broken." Spencer left his crutch in the car. Nothing would keep him from the search. He held Sierra's jacket in front of the dogs' noses. "Find her." Buster knew what he commanded, but Spencer wasn't sure about Annie.

Buster barked and took off, nose to the ground, Annie on his heels.

Spencer left Sierra's purse in the car, but took her coat. Unless Dayton had one wherever he hid out, she'd be cold. Already the temperature hovered around freezing.

The sheriff headed into the woods after the dogs, leaving Spencer to keep up the best he could. His wife glanced back once before stepping out of sight.

Good. The more dogs trying to pick up a scent, the better. He hadn't gone far before his ankle throbbed. Still, he kept going, occasionally leaning against a tree to give his foot a break. As he'd said, nothing was broken but the skin. Nothing severe enough to keep him in town.

He listened for sounds of the dogs. Other than the rustling of trees overhead in the breeze and the scurrying of tiny creatures in the underbrush, the night was silent. A sharp whistle from Westbrook pointed Spencer in the right direction.

"You okay?" The sheriff asked.

"Don't worry about me." He gritted his teeth. "I'll rest my ankle once we have Sierra safe."

"I'm going to take Shadow a ways away," Karlie said. "It's best if we split up."

"Be careful." The sheriff heaved a sigh.

"I know how to take care of myself."

He laughed. "I know you do." He glanced at Spencer. "Someday, I'll tell you how she saved my life by hiding her gun under Shadow's vest."

"Oh, hush. I did what had to be done." Karlie smiled and motioned for Shadow to head in a different direction. Seconds later, the sheriff continued after Buster and Annie.

Obviously, the man did understand how Spencer felt. He saw it in his eyes as his gaze followed his wife into the woods. Spencer got the idea their story might be similar to his and Sierra's in the fact Westbrook had once been terrified out of his mind over the woman he loved. It gave Spencer hope that his and Sierra's story might also have a happy ending.

He continued on, forcing himself past the pain, increasing his pace in order to keep the sheriff in sight. "Hold up."

Westbrook glanced back.

"Your wife is right. We should split up. I'll take Buster, and you keep Annie."

"What about your ankle?"

"I'll live."

The sheriff nodded. "Okay."

Spencer whistled for his dog. When Buster returned to his side, Spencer turned to the left, leaving the sheriff to continue forward. They carried radios to communicate. He'd know immediately if someone found Sierra.

Buster stopped and sniffed the air. With a woof deep in his throat, his hackles raised, he moved more cautiously.

Spencer took the dog's lead and did his best to be as silent as he could with a bad ankle. His gut tightened in anticipation. Adrenaline burned through his veins. They were getting close.

Chapter Nineteen

Snores came from Dayton's sleeping bag. Sierra shook her head. The man actually trusted her to stay put? For a second, she pitied him for the fatal tumor that had changed him.

As slow as possible, she got to her feet, doing her best not to rustle the sleeping bag around her shoulders. She'd freeze without it. She glanced around for Dayton's gun. Seeing it clutched in his hand, she let it be and tip-toed out the front door. The moon lit up the area like a spotlight.

When he made a noise in his sleep, she froze, moving again when he quieted. In front of the shack, she tried to get her bearings. She couldn't take the path they'd taken to get there. That would be the first place Dayton would look when he discovered her gone.

She glanced upward and sent a quick prayer for guidance before turning right. She hadn't gone far before the night split with an inhuman cry. Dayton had woken.

Sierra plunged into the thick woods making enough noise to wake the dead. Once she thought she'd run far enough, she slowed, taking a quieter approach.

A twig snapped behind her. She switched

directions again.

"Sierra!" Dayton roared. "I've no more patience."

The sleeping bag snagged on a bush. The crashing behind her caused Sierra to ditch the bag and run.

The cold bit at her skin, burned her lungs. The hat fell from her head. Not pausing to pick it up, she continued her mad dash to where she hoped to stumble across one of the paths that criss-crossed Misty Mountain.

A dog barked somewhere ahead of her. A cabin or someone searching for her. She glanced behind her and stumbled over a tree root.

She fell sprawled out, the breath knocked from her. Get up! She scrambled back to her feet, ignoring the sting of scraped knees. Her mind started playing tricks on her, she heard breathing right behind her, the pounding of footsteps, all of which came only from herself.

A pain caught in her side. She needed to stop. To rest. She glanced frantically for a hiding place. There. An overhang. She scurried behind it and grabbed a stick the size of her wrist. It would be a better weapon than nothing.

She shivered so hard her teeth clanked together, her chin quivered. He'd hear her for sure. Clamping a hand over her mouth, she peered through the darkness for sight of her pursuer.

Dayton stepped from the shadows, her hat in his hand. "All I ever wanted was for you to love me."

Her grip tightened on the stick.

"To spend what time I had left with me in Mexico. After I was gone, you'd have been very wealthy and free to do as you pleased. Now, you'll have nothing."

He marched past her hiding place and stopped. "Where are you, Sierra? I forgive you. I found your hat. Aren't you cold?"

He switched from angry to sad so fast he gave her whiplash.

"Come out of hiding or I will hunt down Thorne and put a bullet between his eyes."

Sierra snuck from under the overhang and raised the stick. Taking a deep breath, she swung her weapon at his head.

Dayton fell to his knees, then face down on the ground.

Sierra snatched the gun from his hands and fired into the air, emptying the chamber. "I'm sorry, Dayton." She dropped the gun and ran.

An animal burst from the trees.

Sierra screamed, then wrapped her arms around Buster's neck. "Where is Spencer, you beautiful thing." She stood and glanced around. "Spencer!"

"I'm here." He limped from the trees, her coat slung over his arm.

She sprinted toward him and wrapped her arms around his waist.

"Are you okay?" He placed her coat around her.

"Just cold. Dayton is back there. I hit him with a stick."

The sheriff headed toward them, then stopped over Dayton's body. "He's alive." He unclipped handcuffs from his belt and snapped them around Dayton's wrists. "Karlie."

A red-haired woman and her dog stepped onto the path. "I'm here."

"Please take Spencer and Sierra to the station. I

don't think either of them want to ride with this guy."

Dayton stirred and the sheriff hauled him to his feet. "Let's get you some help, Mr. Long."

"It's too late. I'm already dead."

"Then die in peace in a maximum-security hospital." He marched Dayton past them.

Sierra shrank closer to Spencer, her gaze locking with her brother's. So damaged, so hurting, so angry, so confused.

"Come on, Darlin'." Spencer kept her tucked close to his side as they headed after the sheriff and Dayton. "Let's get you warm. What happened to your other clothes?"

"Dayton wanted me dressed in what we wore on our first date. I'm going to burn this dress."

He laughed. "Is this your hat?" He snatched it from Buster's mouth.

"Burn that, too." She smiled up at him. "I am so happy to see you."

"So, where are we going to live? In town or on the mountain?" The corner of his mouth quirked. "Because you are going to marry me, Sierra Wells. I'm not letting you out of my sight again. I love you."

"I love you, too. I guess it's the cabin since I don't own the house I'm in." Warmth spread through her. She'd lived through a harrowing experience and come out better for it with a love and a future. Coming to Misty Hollow hadn't been what she'd envisioned, but it had ended far better than she could have dreamed.

~

Sierra paused in the doorway of Dayton's hospital room. A month had passed since her abduction, and the doctor had notified her that her brother had very little time left. Spencer had driven her to the prison hospital and waited outside while she said goodbye.

The soft hiss of oxygen and the beep of a monitor greeted her. Dayton seemed a shell of himself, so wasted he was from the disease.

She sat in the chair next to his bed. She'd loved him once or so she thought. Having Spencer showed her she hadn't known real love before. Still, this man shared her blood. She'd say goodbye to him as a sister.

His eyelids fluttered open. "Sierra. You came."

"Hello, Dayton. Of course, I did. You're my brother."

Something flickered in his eyes. "So, it's true. We never could have been together."

"No, we couldn't." Tears blurred her vision. "You'll have to settle for the love a sister." She took his hand, the skin so thin she could count the veins.

"I'll take what I can. I'm sorry for…everything."

"Oh, I know." She'd worked every day on saying her next words and actually believed them to be true. At least at that moment. There would be many more battles ahead for her to stay true to the fact she forgave him. "I forgive you."

Tears ran down the sides of his face. "I don't deserve that, but thank you."

She leaned over and kissed his cheek. "Goodbye, Dayton." She stood and marched from the room and back to Spencer, ending one chapter of her life and beginning another.

The End

Enjoy the first chapter of Calm Surface.

DECEPTIVE PEACE

Chapter One

Maddy Everton inserted the key into the lock of the house that had once belonged to her sister, Allison. Tears sprang to her eyes. Only a month had passed since Allison's murder, her body discovered in Lake Misty, and the house already smelled of mildew.

"Don't worry, little sister. I'll find out who did this to you." Maddy headed back to her car to unload the suitcases from the trunk.

When she'd received the call from the Misty Hollow police department that her sister's body had been discovered, she'd quit her job in Oak Ridge and taken a teaching job in Misty Hollow. She hadn't thought twice about coming to find out what had happened to Alli.

Who would want to kill such a sweet girl? At twenty-three, her sister had come to this town on a quest for independence. A town where she could forge her own life. The last time Maddy had spoken to her, Alli had been over the moon about her new job at the local library. She'd used her inheritance from their parents to purchase the little two-bedroom house in town that would now be Maddy's home for however long it took.

She heaved the largest suitcase from the trunk and

glanced around. On each side of her was a white house with a wraparound porch. Country charm that belied a town that housed evil. Oh, she knew of the troubles Misty Hollow had had in the past. She'd done her research before coming. Sweet and peaceful, seemingly calm, but this hidden little town could be a cauldron of trouble.

A quick glance at her watch alerted her that she'd arrived later than she'd wanted. That was her, Miss Perpetually Late. Meet the teacher night at the school started in four hours, and she still hadn't prepared her classroom. She slid the suitcases just inside the front door, then sped to the local elementary school.

"You must be Madison Everton." A smiling woman a few years older than Maddy pulled a box from Maddy's trunk. I'm Susan Snodgrass. I also teach fifth grade. You'll want to check in with the principal and secretary before heading to your room. Meanwhile, I can ask the maintenance man to unload your car for you."

"Really?" Maddy grinned. "That would be great. I've just arrived in town."

"Wow. You're really pushing it."

"Yep." She rushed into the building, greeted everyone she needed to greet, then got hopelessly lost trying to find her room. "Ah. Room 105." As promised, all her boxes sat in her room. She wouldn't have time to set up the room exactly as she wanted it, but she'd make a good effort.

A man in navy-blue coveralls leaned against her door frame. His eyes narrowed. "Everton? You related to the girl the police just found in the lake?"

Maddy stiffened. "I'm her sister. You are?"

"Gene Howard. Site specialist. Welcome to Misty Hollow. I hope you find what you're looking for. But I also hope you aren't bringing trouble with you." Before she could thank him for bringing in her boxes, he left.

Despite his greeting, she didn't feel welcomed in the slightest. She quickly slid books into bookcases, slapped up a few encouraging posters, and set out a few personal items on her desk. That's the best she could do. Tomorrow would be more productive as long as meetings didn't fill up all her time.

"Folks are arriving. You ready?" Susan poked her head into the room.

"As ready as I'll ever be." Maddy fought to control her racing heart. She should've arrived in town yesterday, but it had taken longer to find a renter for her apartment in Oak Ridge than she'd thought. She took up position outside her classroom door and pasted on a welcoming smile. As a second-year teacher, she knew the drill.

A handsome man strolled the halls. What made him stand out was the fact he didn't have a student with him. Had the school asked for extra security for that night?

He caught her watching and headed her way. "Hello. You're new."

"Maddy Everton."

A flicker crossed his eyes. "Family to Allison Everton?"

"Her sister." Maddy hitched her chin. "I'm here to find out what happened to her."

His smile faded. "That could be very dangerous, ma'am."

She shrugged, keeping her smile in place as she

turned to greet a man and young boy. "Will you be in my class this year? I'm Miss Everton."

The boy nodded.

"Speak up, Danny." The man with him placed a hand on the boy's shoulders. "I'm Ryan Maxwell. This is my nephew, Danny. He lives with me." His gaze flicked to the other man. "Bundt. I didn't know you were working tonight."

"Last minute." Deputy Bundt smirked. "With you off for this event, we're left a bit short-handed."

"Mr. Maxwell, perhaps you and Danny would like to see the room?" she intervened. The tension between the two men could be cut with a chainsaw.

They stepped into her room. Maddy motioned to the seat Danny would be occupying. She'd placed a new notebook and pencil at each desk.

Mr. Maxwell asked the same question everyone else seemed to ask. "You related to Allison Everton?"

Maddy exhaled heavily. "Yes, sir. I'm her sister." Her gaze clashed with his dark one. "I'm here to find out who killed her."

~

Was the woman insane? He started to say something to that effect but stopped as Danny glanced their way.

When Danny browsed through the books on the shelf, Ryan lowered his voice. "Your sister was murdered, Miss Everton. Let the police handle finding out what happened."

"We know what happened." She crossed her arms. "Someone murdered her after keeping her hidden for a few days, then dumped her in the lake like fish guts."

A harsh but effective analogy. "If you get in the

way of the sheriff's department, you will be arrested." He gave her a firm nod, then called for Danny to follow him.

"I think my new teacher will be nice," his nephew said. "She's pretty. Don't you think so?"

Blond ponytail that hung to her waist and flashing hazel eyes? Yes, she was very pretty. She also looked very much like her deceased sister. "I'm sure you'll like it in Misty Hollow."

"Won't you?" Danny glanced up at him. "It's smaller than Langley. You won't get shot at as much. I like the mountain and the lake. It's nice here."

Ryan ruffled the boy's hair. "Good point." Hopefully, the reason Ryan accepted the position with the Misty Hollow sheriff's office would prove wrong. But with the death of pretty, blond Allison and the circumstances surrounding her death, he didn't think so.

They ran into Deputy Bundt again when Danny wanted to see the multi-purpose room. The lawman was speaking with a man in blue coveralls. Another man leaned against a far wall, his sharp gaze on everyone that came into the large room.

Where was that man's kid? Ryan narrowed his eyes, everyone a suspect. Against another wall, someone had set up a long table with cookies and lemonade. Danny made a beeline for the snacks and struck up a conversation with a boy around his age.

The man lounging against the wall looked interested when Miss Everton entered, but the boy Danny spoke to called him, diverting his attention. Ryan shook off his suspicions. The new teacher was beautiful. Every man in the place glanced her way. That didn't mean one of them was a killer.

Except his belief the killer lived in Misty Hollow had brought Ryan here. He'd bide his time and pray he was wrong.

Miss Everton marched toward Bundt. From her posture, he guessed she was asking questions about the investigation into her sister's death.

"I'll be right over here, Danny. You can see me."

His nephew rolled his eyes. "I'm not a baby."

"No, you're not. Sorry for treating you like one." Ryan joined Bundt and the teacher in time to hear him say he couldn't divulge that information.

"Miss Everton." Ryan squared his shoulders. "I understand your drive to find answers, but you should know that the authorities can't give you much information."

Her lovely eyes darted from one lawman to the other. "I feel as if I'm being ganged up on."

He frowned. "How so?"

"Deputy Bundt and I were having a conversation, then you come over and start issuing orders."

"He *is* the captain," Bundt said with a smirk. "I'm the grunt, along with Deputy Miller."

Ryan knew why the other man disliked him so much. He'd heard how Bundt had been handling the duties of captain before Ryan arrived on the scene. Now, he answered to Ryan, and they'd be spending time together solving the murder of a young woman well-liked by most in Misty Hollow.

"Are you staying in your sister's house, Miss Everton?" He glanced at the teacher.

"Yes. Please call me Maddy. Everyone does. Only the students will call me Miss Everton." She tilted her head. "There's no reason for me to stay anywhere else when my sister's place is vacant." A shadow crossed her features. "There might be something there to help me find out who killed her. Isn't it usually someone who knew the victim?"

"Not necessarily." Especially if Ryan's suspicion was right. Serial killers didn't usually know their victims.

"I'll let you two argue. Have a nice evening, Miss…Maddy." Bundt strode from the room.

"Is he the school resource officer?" Maddy asked. "Otherwise, why would law enforcement be here tonight?"

"Nothing better to do."

She arched a brow. "Things seemed quite hot this time last year."

"You've done your homework."

"Of course. Then, before that, the sheriff and his present wife had their own adventure. Misty Hollow isn't the charming small town people think it is."

"All towns have their share of trouble." *This* woman was going to be trouble. He had no doubt.

~

His hands itched to grab the pretty new teacher. But, he'd have to bide his time. He already had a woman to love and three days to convince her to love him back. He'd taken her from the grocery store two hours ago, then came here.

Not to show up on Meet the Teacher Night would look suspicious. Everyone in town came. The start of a new school year was a party to most of them, even those without children in the school. The people of Misty Hollow grabbed at any chance to break the monotony of routine. From his shady spot in the parking lot, he waited and watched until the blond teacher headed for her car. He'd follow her home, watch her go inside, then head to where his new woman waited for him.

Dear Reader,

I hope you enjoyed the second book in the Misty Hollow series. If so, please leave a review. Reviews are priceless to an author and help new readers discover their books.

Sierra and Dayton's story is a little different from most you might have read. When I started writing this story, I focused only on the fact that Sierra's mother kept secret that she'd given a child up for adoption. The story took off, choosing its own direction. What could shake someone up more than finding out the man they almost married was their brother? Then, add in the brain tumor that made him turn into someone he wasn't only added to the suspense.

What in the world will happen in Calm Surface?

God Bless,

Cynthia Hickey.

Did you miss Secrets of Misty Hollow, book one? Take a peek.

Chapter One

"Bye, Mom." Karlie Marshall darted out the cabin door and rushed to her late model Toyota Tacoma. If she didn't hurry, she'd be late, again, for her shift as a waitress at Misty Hollow Diner. Her mom's words about being careful followed her across the yard.

Always the worrier, her mother. Quiet, content to work in her garden or fish the nearby lake, her mom stayed to herself, more than happy to sit at home when she wasn't working at the town's small library. Not Karlie. She loved her small town but wanted—no, needed—to visit a sprawling city. A place with more than the thirty thousand Shakerville had.

It almost wasn't worth the long drive just to buy something she couldn't find locally. Plus, whenever she mentioned leaving, her mother would almost have a heart attack. At twenty-five, it was past time for Karlie to make her own way. The problem was…she didn't know what she wanted. She loved Misty Hollow but craved a little more excitement than the small town had to offer.

The whoop whoop of a siren sounded behind her.

Karlie glanced in her rearview mirror to see the blinking red and blue lights of a police car, then down at the speedometer. Ugh. Speeding again. She doubted she'd get away with a warning this time. She watched an officer approach in her side-view mirror. Not a familiar face. Was this the new sheriff everyone was talking about?

He tapped on the window. "License and registration, please."

Sighing, Karlie rolled down her window, then reached over to open the glove compartment. "I'm sorry, Sheriff. I was speeding. I'm late for work."

"Later now." His lips twitched. He took the documents and returned to his SUV.

Karlie leaned her head against the steering wheel. Idiot. She jerked upright as the sheriff returned. "You're new?"

"Sheriff Westbrook, at your service." He handed her back her documents, then a ticket.

"You're giving me a ticket?" Her voice rose.

"You were going fifteen miles over the speed limit, ma'am."

Her shoulders slumped. "Fine." She shoved the ticket into her purse. "Welcome to Misty Hollow." When he stepped back, she sped away, careful to only go five miles over the limit. She'd have to work overtime to pay for the ticket.

If she weren't so angry, and late, she'd dwell on how handsome the new sheriff was even with the reflective sunglasses he wore. Dark blond hair, chiseled chin with just a hint of a dimple. Too bad.

Darn. Her speed had crept up again.

She glanced in her rearview mirror. Was he

following her? She slowed and took the turn into town.

"Sorry." She rushed to the back to put her purse in her locker. "I got pulled over for speeding."

"Bound to happen sooner or later with the way you drive." The owner, Myrtle McIlroy shook her head. "Maybe I should put you down for half an hour earlier every day so you'll arrive when you're actually supposed to."

Karlie laughed, then noticed her boss's new hair color. "Nice. Makes you look like Lucille Ball."

"Stop the flattery and get to work. We're already busy with the morning rush." She waved a dish towel in Karlie's direction. "The other girl called in sick. I've been busier than a one-armed paper hanger."

Karlie grabbed her apron and a menu as the bell over the diner door jingled. She rushed out and skid to a halt as the new sheriff entered. She swallowed when he smiled her way. "Just one?"

He nodded, removing his sunglasses to reveal hazel eyes. "Yes, ma'am."

"It's Karlie. Follow me, please." She led him to a booth. "I know cops like to be able to see all exits. Hope this will suffice."

"It will." He set his hat on the table and took his seat.

"Coffee?" Karlie handed him a menu.

"Please." The dimple in his cheek deepened. "Newspaper?"

She left and returned with both, her gaze landing on the front page. "Who's Anthony Bartelloni?" She motioned to the story of a man being released from prison.

"Mob boss. He was released on probation. Should

have stayed locked up for a very long time. I'll have the breakfast special."

Karlie placed the order and hurried to serve another customer, then glanced at the paper. The article said that Bartelloni had skipped out of town, left New York for parts unknown. She'd never heard the name before, but mobs were dangerous, right? She'd read about them in books.

"Table four's up," Myrtle called.

Karlie placed another order and carried the sheriff's food to him. "Let me know if you need anything else."

"How do you like Misty Hollow?"

"It's okay. A bit boring, and everyone knows everything about everyone else. Gossip is the favorite pastime." She smiled. "You arrived a couple of days ago, right?"

He nodded. "Looking forward to a slower pace."

"I'd say you've been busy already. Who tickets people before nine a.m.?" She arched a brow over flashing blue eyes, her smile fading. "Enjoy your breakfast." She marched away.

~

Yes, Heath had been busy. He knew exactly who Karlie Marshall was. Also knew who she used to be. With Bartelloni's whereabouts unknown, Heath had been filled in on the possible danger to Karlie and her mother. The challenge would be keeping them safe without revealing their true identities. He was counting on the Misty Hollow gossip chain to let him know if any strangers arrived in town.

Karlie's laugh drew his attention to the pretty redhead. Imagine his surprise when he realized the identity of the woman he'd ticketed that morning. Heath hadn't expected to meet her so soon upon arriving in Misty Hollow. He'd been told that Sharon Marshall was a bit of a recluse and figured the daughter was as well.

Orders had been to make friends with the Marshall women. He wasn't off to a very good start. He read through the newspaper article. There wasn't much to go on. The FBI feared someone had leaked information about the women, but whether Bartelloni knew exactly where they were was unknown. So, erring on the side of caution, Heath went undercover as the new sheriff. He glanced out the window at the trees and vintage brick buildings. Staying here wouldn't be a hardship. It sure beat the concrete jungle of the city.

Breakfast finished, he left a hefty tip and headed to the register to pay for his meal and the paper. "Give the chef my compliments," he told Karlie.

"Myrtle, the sheriff said the food was good," she turned and called through the pass-thru window.

A middle-aged woman with bright orange hair popped up and grinned. "Thank you, Sheriff. Come again."

"I'll be a regular, most likely." He nodded and left, heading for his car. He'd been on the mountain to familiarize himself with the area around the Marshall home. Now, he intended to drive the other mountain roads to acquaint himself with empty places a man could hide. The area was so wooded sneaking up on a home would be easy.

His radio beeped. "Sheriff Westbrook."

"Sheriff, we've a call of a domestic situation on Coon Road," his receptionist, Annie, said.

"On my way." He punched the address into his GPS and sped toward the address.

A rundown trailer sat in the middle of what looked like a junkyard, but was more the result of hoarding. A pit bull barked and pulled against the chain holding him to a tree. Heath unclipped his gun holster, ready to shoot if the dog broke loose and charged. Loud voices came from inside the trailer. Heath beeped the horn and exited his SUV.

A man stepped onto a sagging porch. "What?"

"We've had a call about a disturbance."

"From who? We ain't got no neighbors." The man's stomach stretched the limits of a stained tee shirt.

"Is your wife home?"

"Sally, get your butt out here. The sheriff wants to talk to you."

A woman, as thin as the man was pudgy, joined him on the porch. "Shut up, Brute," she hollered at the dog. "I can't hear myself think." She crossed her arms. "What can I do for you, Sheriff?"

"Everything all right here?" He glanced from one to the other. Who'd called the sheriff's department? A hunter, maybe? The man was right. There were no neighbors within hearing distance.

"You might have to arrest me," she said. "I'm about to beat my husband's head in."

"Let's not do that. What's the problem?"

"She's mad because I sold some of her scrap metal to buy beer." The man rolled his eyes. "Look at this place. How'd she know anything was missing?"

How indeed? Heath warned them about keeping things civil and returned to his vehicle. If it had been a hunter who made the call, they were hunting illegally.

His day just got busier. He drove down a little-used path called a road and parked next to Misty Hollow Lake. A red-haired woman fished from the bank. Sharon Marshall.

She turned as he cut off the engine. "Howdy, Sheriff."

"Ma'am. Did you place a call to the station about a disturbance?"

"Yes. They were disturbing the peace, and I feared someone would be injured." Worry crossed the woman who looked like an older version of Karlie.

"Just an argument. Getting any bites?"

She bent over and lifted a string from the water. "Three bass. Enough for supper."

He wanted to warn her not to go out alone. To stay home. But, without solid proof that Bartelloni knew where she was, making her afraid seemed wrong.

"Why don't you come by for supper?" She smiled. "There'll be plenty." She gave him her address. "It's always nice to make friends with the local authorities."

Smart woman. Making friends meant local law enforcement would keep a closer eye on their friend. Would she change her mind when she heard he'd ticketed her daughter? "I'd love to. See you later, ma'am."

By the end of his workday, Heath looked forward to a home-cooked meal. Eating out became old after a while, and he wanted a chance to see the Marshalls in their home. Determine, if possible, how defenseless they might be.

He changed into jeans and a button-up shirt, shoved his feet into cowboy boots, packed his things and then checked out of the motel. He climbed into his

SUV, radio clipped to his belt. He might be officially off work, but his job never really ended at five o'clock. Not in such a small town where the station held him and two others.

Heath pulled into the graveled drive of the Marshall place and studied the cleared lawn. As with most of the homes out of the town limits, woods surrounded the house on three sides. Someone had cleared a nice space for a lawn and a garden. But this place gave a new meaning to the word, remote. A good thing when in the Witness Protection program. Bad if someone you'd wronged wanted to get to you—

On the porch, he raised his hand to knock and stopped as Karlie's voice rose inside.

"Mom, why does the DNA test I got back today show that I'm the daughter of Anthony Bartelloni?"

Website at *www.cynthiahickey.com*

www.cynthiahickey.com

Multi-published and best-selling author, Cynthia Hickey, has taught writing at many conferences and small writing retreats. She and her husband run the publishing press, Winged Publications, which includes some of the CBA's best well-known authors. They live in Arizona and Arkansas, becoming snowbirds with two dogs and one cat. They have ten grandchildren who them busy and tell everyone they know that "Nana is a writer."

Connect with me on *FaceBook*
Twitter
Sign up for my *newsletter and receive a free short story*
www.cynthiahickey.com

Follow me on *Amazon*
And *Bookbub*

Enjoy other books by Cynthia Hickey

CLEAN BUT GRITTY Romantic Suspense

Highland Springs

Murder Live
Say Bye to Mommy
To Breathe Again
Highland Springs Murders (all 3 in one)

Colors of Evil Series

Shades of Crimson
Coral Shadows

The Pretty Must Die Series

Ripped in Red, book 1
Pierced in Pink, book 2
Wounded in White, book 3
Worthy, The Complete Story

Lisa Paxton Mystery Series

Eenie Meenie Miny Mo
Jack Be Nimble
Hickory Dickory Dock

DECEPTIVE PEACE

The Portal

The Tail Waggin' Mysteries
Cat-Eyed Witness
The Dog Who Found a Body
Troublesome Twosome
Four-Legged Suspect
Unwanted Christmas Guest

Tiny House Mysteries
No Small Caper
Caper Goes Missing
Caper Finds a Clue
Caper's Dark Adventure
A Strange Game for Caper
Caper Steals Christmas
Caper Finds a Treasure
Tiny House Mysteries boxed set

Wife for Hire – Private Investigators
Saving Sarah
Lesson for Lacey
Mission for Meghan
Long Way for Lainie
Aimed at Amy
Wife for Hire (all five in one)

A Hollywood Murder
Killer Pose, book 1

Killer Snapshot, book 2
Shoot to Kill, book 3
Kodak Kill Shot, book 4
To Snap a Killer
Hollywood Murder Mysteries

Shady Acres Mysteries
Beware the Orchids, book 1
Path to Nowhere
Poison Foliage
Poinsettia Madness
Deadly Greenhouse Gases
Vine Entrapment
Shady Acres Boxed Set

Overcoming Evil series
Mistaken Assassin
Captured Innocence
Mountain of Fear
Exposure at Sea
A Secret to Die for
Collision Course
Romantic Suspense of 5 books in 1

INSPIRATIONAL

Nosy Neighbor Series
Anything For A Mystery, Book 1

A Killer Plot, Book 2
Skin Care Can Be Murder, Book 3
Death By Baking, Book 4
Jogging Is Bad For Your Health, Book 5
Poison Bubbles, Book 6
A Good Party Can Kill You, Book 7
Nosy Neighbor collection

Christmas with Stormi Nelson

The Summer Meadows Series
Fudge-Laced Felonies, Book 1
Candy-Coated Secrets, Book 2
Chocolate-Covered Crime, Book 3
Maui Macadamia Madness, Book 4
All four novels in one collection

The River Valley Mystery Series
Deadly Neighbors, Book 1
Advance Notice, Book 2
The Librarian's Last Chapter, Book 3
All three novels in one collection

Historical cozy
Hazel's Quest

Historical Romances
Runaway Sue

CYNTHIA HICKEY

Taming the Sheriff
Sweet Apple Blossom
A Doctor's Agreement
A Lady Maid's Honor
A Touch of Sugar
Love Over Par
Heart of the Emerald
A Sketch of Gold
Her Lonely Heart

Finding Love the Harvey Girl Way
Cooking With Love
Guiding With Love
Serving With Love
Warring With Love
All 4 in 1

Finding Love in Disaster
The Rancher's Dilemma
The Teacher's Rescue
The Soldier's Redemption

Woman of courage Series

A Love For Delicious
Ruth's Redemption
Charity's Gold Rush
Mountain Redemption
They Call Her Mrs. Sheriff

Woman of Courage series

Short Story Westerns
Desert Rose
Desert Lilly
Desert Belle
Desert Daisy
Flowers of the Desert 4 in 1

Contemporary

Romance in Paradise
Maui Magic
Sunset Kisses
Deep Sea Love
3 in 1

Finding a Way Home
Service of Love
Hillbilly Cinderella
Unraveling Love
I'd Rather Kiss My Horse

Christmas
Dear Jillian
Romancing the Fabulous Cooper Brothers
Handcarved Christmas
The Payback Bride
Curtain Calls and Christmas Wishes
Christmas Gold

CYNTHIA HICKEY

A Christmas Stamp
Snowflake Kisses
Merry's Secret Santa
A Christmas Deception

The Red Hat's Club (Contemporary novellas)

Finally
Suddenly
Surprisingly
The Red Hat's Club 3 – in 1

Short Story

One Hour (A short story thriller)
Whisper Sweet Nothings (a Valentine short romance)

Made in the USA
Monee, IL
16 November 2023